About the Author

Michael James, aka Mike Simpson, is a retired English teacher with an ingenious and inquisitive mind who lives with his wife in East Molesey, Surrey – children having fled. He has written two books for children and two immensely popular novels for adults. Ghost writing for sportsmen and business entrepreneurs has probably prevented many other fine books being completed. The assignments fun and enlightening. In this new book, he has been prompted by the mysterious disappearance of a local woman in suspicious circumstances.

The Remains of Stephanie Gayle

Michael James

The Remains of Stephanie Gayle

Olympia Publishers
London

www.olympiapublishers.com
OLYMPIA PAPERBACK EDITION

Copyright © Michael James 2024

The right of Michael James to be identified as author of
this work has been asserted in accordance with sections 77 and 78 of
the Copyright, Designs and Patents Act 1988.

All Rights Reserved

No reproduction, copy or transmission of this publication
may be made without written permission.
No paragraph of this publication may be reproduced,
copied or transmitted save with the written permission of the publisher,
or in accordance with the provisions
of the Copyright Act 1956 (as amended).

Any person who commits any unauthorised act in relation to
this publication may be liable to criminal
prosecution and civil claims for damage.

A CIP catalogue record for this title is
available from the British Library.

ISBN: 978-1-80439-609-4

This is a work of fiction.
Names, characters, places and incidents originate from the writer's
imagination. Any resemblance to actual persons, living or dead, is
purely coincidental.

First Published in 2024

Olympia Publishers
Tallis House
2 Tallis Street
London
EC4Y 0AB

Printed in Great Britain

Dedication

Dedicated to my children, Louise and Hannah.

Acknowledgements

Thanks to Dave Jevons and Phil Lo for the nudges and suggestions.

Chapter One

At every mirror, in every room that had one, she looked. She looked at the lines, at the creases, at the blemishes, at the dark bags under her eyes and the heavy hoods above them. She ran her fingers across her forehead, following each furrow in her brow. She pulled at the dry, lifeless hair. So much fury and sadness had taken its toll.

The house was heavy with warmth; wood burner blazed in the front room, the lounge and the central heating pumped extra cosiness throughout her comfortable home. Autumn allowed such satisfaction indoors. Somehow the garden was closed for the coming winter and a form of hibernation had begun.

A mumbling television rumbled away, comfort but not concern. And, waiting patiently, a glass of rich scarlet wine, breathing, near her usual dent in the sofa.

Kirsty Foster walked her territory. Kitchen and utility tidied, reception rooms spick and span and hallway inviting. Everything was in its place and had been carefully dressed. She was a proud housekeeper. Habitually she pulled herself up the stairs, wiping her finger along the banisters, checking for invading dust. At each bedroom door she stood for a while to listen.

Kirsty's three gorgeous children slept. From the youngest child's room came the contented murmurs of deep slumber. Charlie was a good sleeper, and he had spent the day charging round the fading garden and clambering up and over the climbing frame that his father had recently constructed under his son's eager and excitable gesticulations.

Safe and almost soundless, Kirsty's eight year old, Justine, hugged her pillow with a mere soft whistle to accompany her dreams; most probably of dancing or drawing. Next door, her 'just older' brother, Elliot, trumpeted indistinctly, and his feet shuffled and dislodged bedding as he scored yet another goal or sailed for gold.

With satisfaction at the conclusion of this ritual, Kirsty paused at another mirror, found the lines hadn't disappeared and ventured downstairs to be ambushed by the welcoming wine.

The fortress was secure and seemingly all was in order, but that was physical. Nagging her every woken hour, infesting her fractured sleep and gnawing her fragile guts was a loss that routine and time refused to heal.

Alcohol helped, a little. The children and their demands helped, a little. Some casual friendships allowed a brief respite. Her husband's absence didn't help at all.

One glass of moderately pleasant wine was never enough, and there had been times when one bottle had been totally inadequate. Kirsty plodded to the kitchen and grabbed the bottle. And that is when she heard it again. She braked sharply, gritted her teeth and clenched her eyes. He was back. She knew what it meant. Felt the folds and furrows of her face deepen. Her bowels tighten.

Slow and definite came long scratching. As if claws were being run down the window of the French doors. Several times, repeated for her terror, came the scraping. Kirsty could not move. The enticing wine was even forgotten. Her brow moist, her frame shaking.

Whenever he came to torment her, it was different. A shed

door left to creak all night, a creosote stain on the lawn, broken egg on the patio, stones arranged into a cross, washing line cut; there had been many. But nothing she could take to the police, nothing much that her 'oh so rational' husband would believe. And as usual, her 'oh so always fucking absent' husband was thousands of painful miles away at an emerging oilfield in Nigeria.

Kirsty didn't notice when the scratching stopped. It had probably been fleeting, but it seemed like several minutes. And it was several more minutes or even a whole hour before she prised her damp body from the chair. The first thing to grab was the powerful torch that Tom had left for her. She could ignite the far end of the garden and others nearby with that beast.

At the window, she rubbed at the glass as if it helped. It didn't. Much of the beam of torchlight reflected in the glazing until she pushed it hard against the window. Nothing was happening. All seemed as it should be. Again and again she waved the slicing light across the grass, up and down the patio, in and out of the bushes; as if searching for night bombers in the Blitz.

With a certain degree of relief, Kirsty made one last sweep, ready to put the torch to bed, when she spotted something unexpected, outwardly of little significance. Two small white shapes. Pieces of paper stuck against the paving slabs. She aimed at them, but with little joy as the brilliance of the light simply reflected back. Her mind cranked up and a litany of ideas rattled through her head. She was too curious to leave it until daylight.

Singing as she went. Long strides and fixed determination. No one would be there. It was safe. Kirsty bent down and studied the pieces of white paper. They were damp. She peeled the small sheets off the stone, held them in the palm of her hand and hurried back indoors.

Photographs, or at least that's what they looked like, but cheap photocopies, now rippled and tacky with the wet. Kirsty peered incredulously at the pictures. Slowly she pulled the two together. It had been one sheet and torn roughly down the middle. She gulped. Her hand trembled. Both eyes felt as if they would detach. Kirsty clenched her lips tightly and whimpered. Staring up at her were the gleeful faces of her two younger children, their faces cut in two by the rip. Faces from what seemed to be an old school photograph.

Kirsty curled up, foetal. Her whole body cradled, trembling.

Chapter Two

Children are often able to detect when things are not how they were, or how they should be. Charlie, Justine and Elliot knew their mother was struggling at breakfast. She hardly spoke, eyes looking beyond the children. Dark, haunted eyes searching into a far distance. Now Kirsty didn't yell. She always yelled. Kirsty didn't straighten uniforms. Kirsty always straightened uniforms. Lunch boxes rattled and crackled with packaged stuff. There wasn't the heavy sliding of well-prepared and wholesome sandwiches. An unpleasant silence that none of the children felt ready to break.

Everything followed the routine and assumed pattern. There had been mornings like this before, and these children knew how to play it. They huddled in the hallway; Kirsty grabbed a coat and hung on to car keys.

'Ready? Let's go.' A sharp bark. 'Got everything?' Brief and brittle words. It was all she could manage.

Each child was duly delivered. Kirsty forced a painful smile goodbye.

And when she returned, she was more than ready to stand there. To stand there like she had so many times. To stand outside Craig Gayle's bleak detached home. Just stand there. So Gayle could see her. Make him unsure of her intentions. Outside the house where she had spent numerous blissful times with her inseparable friend, Stephanie. Knowing her soul mate wouldn't be coming home.

Stephanie, Stephanie, Stephanie. How it hurt. How it had been hurting for four agonising years. Stephanie had disappeared four years ago. Just vanished. Whoosh. Gone. No money or cards, no clothes, no passport, no explanation. Spirits high. Leaving five young children that she loved. A birthday on the horizon, children off to a concert. How she had adored those kids. No word to her true buddy. Kirsty's stomach churned; because Kirsty knew. And what she knew tortured her every waking, and sleeping, hour. So, she stood outside the house. Outside the house of Stephanie's killer. That Craig Gayle had killed her was unarguable. Kirsty never doubted.

There was no movement from the building, now heavily curtained and noticeably grimier than before. Kirsty hoped he was peeking through the narrowest gap at the window. Hoping he would see her. Without any doubt, it was Craig Gayle who had been at the back of her house, had last night scratched at her window and left the torn photographs. Her campaign was getting to him. She was hoping he was cracking.

Without Tom, stuck out on the edge of the Sahara, she was a lonely individual. There were even times she talked to herself to make sure she hadn't lost the art of conversation. Sure she exchanged something like pleasantries with other mothers at the school gates, but she was quick to snatch the children up and escape. He might be there. Some Gayle children were still at the same school. Still in the same class. She couldn't stop that. Kirsty pulled at her hair. All of the children in the same photograph.

Fortunately, it wasn't raining, and Kirsty leant against a shedding ash tree across the street from the Gayle house. She knew every room and every colour of every wall. Craig Gayle hadn't changed a thing since Stephanie had gone. Parties, coffee mornings, just popping in to gossip, dropping the kids, feeding the cat; Kirsty was more family than visitor. These were delicious times. Her friendship with Stephanie was deeper than just being a mate, a chum, a pal. They understood each other. Loved, not in a sordid way, each other.

Now a dreadful emptiness. A whacking great space. Kirsty found it hard to grieve. She supposed she was still in shock. Most people have a body to mourn. Sometimes there is graphic carnage. It was not like a bloody slaughter, a battered carcass. A door was wide open and no matter how she tried, close it she couldn't. There had been funerals of others; relations, distant friends. At all these, in Kirsty's head, only Stephanie's corpse was in the casket, pale and cold; so very cold.

Abruptly from her reverie, she jumped, alert. A movement at a bedroom window, a definite brush of the curtain. Only momentarily and then nothing.

Searching in her head to reach a memory. Why had it been three days before he had reported Stephanie missing? Three days. So much you can do in three days. She wouldn't have left without telling Kirsty. There had been problems, but if she had been organising an escape, Kirsty would have certainly been on the planning committee. No, she would have never abandoned the kids. She worshipped them. Untidy and dysfunctional at times, but those children were her salvation and her sanity in a rocky marriage.

At the time of Stephanie's disappearance, it was frenetic. Kirsty had been the dynamo, the energy behind finding her great friend. At crazy times she had walked the streets and chatted with strangers. Quite ingenious for Kirsty, she had used a recent photo of Stephanie and delivered a 'missing' leaflet to houses locally. Craig Gayle had been by her side, but a limp addition to Kirsty's crusade. Knowing that Stephanie had often frequented New Covent Garden with Craig, in her madness Kirsty had gone to the market with him and avidly handed out the flyer to traders and punters. A desperate woman. And all the time, but not that Kirsty was originally aware, Craig Gayle sat back during this intense period. Not waiting, it would seem, for his wife to return, but for the furore to die down. Even the buzzing Kirsty, slowly but surely, recognised Gayle's understandable lack of enthusiasm for the task. Dark clouds of suspicion often drift slowly down, and you piece together, with jigsaw accuracy, a despicable alternative. Manoeuvring her black agenda, Kirsty had, before long, established the fate of her dearest friend. Craig Gayle was, in fact, behind his wife's apparent vanishing act.

Of course, he was quizzed by the police. He was a depressed man, but not a killer. An initial arrest. It was a procedure. He came up with lame explanations; he thought there was an affair, she'd run off with a gardener or the plumber, would come back, a minor tiff. Kirsty was now fully convinced that Craig Gayle was guilty. As the weeks dragged on, there was no move to charge him, despite some anxious calls by Kirsty to the officers who were orchestrating the case. Eventually, she decided that the police were sure of his guilt but didn't have the evidence to convict him. And it would be cosier and cheaper, especially with five kids to consider, that the killer stayed free, unlikely to harm anyone else, and a family wouldn't be split up. Save a lot of time and money. Sometimes, the law embraces conveniences like this.

Kirsty shivered. It could have been the fresh breeze that now whipped round the skeletal tree. It was more likely the horrors in her head. Reinforced by the small pieces of dog-eared paper deep in her pocket that she stroked with her fingers; two scraps of a photograph that she knew Craig Gayle had intimidated her with, prodded her vulnerability. Kirsty needed a journey, a journey back in her treasured memory that could lighten the load. And as she stood in the gloomy shadows of a killer's house, Kirsty's head drifted, curling out of reality, to embrace the essence of her friend.

*

It was as if she was bringing her to life. Raising Stephanie from the pitiful grave her husband had assigned her. Her same charismatic friend bouncing back once more. A warm afternoon conjured up brought it all back. One they had spent with the kids, on a grassy ridge in the undulating Surrey Hills. Stephanie was laughing loudly; a warm, intoxicating chortle that was her signature expression. And accompanying her raucous snigger was a wide-eyed beaming smile. The Stephanie of Kirsty's reverie was breathing perfection, peering into the picnic basket that Kirsty had filled for a day out to Leith Hill. Sandwiches and drinks, pies and cake, plastic cutlery and battered cups were bundled haphazardly in the wicker hamper. There were sarcastic comments that were warm and humorous, not cutting and hostile. The hamper was a car crash; both Stephanie and Kirsty could see that. Stephanie called it Kirsty's jumble sale selection.

Flapping in the still air of summer was the large tartan blanket Stephanie had donated to this hilltop meal. The first of many embedded memories of that day. Kirsty held steadfast to her side of the blanket, and Stephanie as equally firm to the other. Recognising the possibilities first one of the kids' football was heaved up in the air using this blanket, to the squealing amusement of both children and adults. Harmless, unfettered fun. That was until it was suggested that young Charlie might enjoy the delights of flight. Gently and without the vigour of tossing the ball, Charlie was hoisted upwards and carefully grounded, much to his gleeful excitement.

With the youngsters running wildly through copses of trees and rolling in the summer grass, Stephanie had pulled out the chilled wine and chinked beakers, to all the fine things in life, with Kirsty. They spoke of this idyllic setting, of the fine weather, the children's happiness and then the darkening cracks in Stephanie's marriage. Kirsty herself was hanging on to the fluctuating fortunes of living with a much-absent Tom, which may well have been the 'air' she needed. Partnerships can be stifling. Stephanie's was suffocating. There was a list for Craig Gayle that Stephanie bombarded Kirsty with. The four children they shared should bond a couple, but the adhesion was splitting of this marriage, mere fragments remaining. Stephanie told of her flings with the gardener and the plumber. How tedious her marriage to Craig had become. His violence, his greed; hanging on to what she thought both possessed. There were only splinters left of what had once been a fulfilled partnership.

One by one, puffing over-heated, over-exercised children flopped down on the now rumpled blanket, ready to be fed. Kirsty dealt out a baffling variety of sagging sandwiches and crumpled crisp packets, soon to be followed by squished chocolate puddings as pulverised as their plastic containers.

Taking over were the heroics of tree climbing. It was the new 'best ever' experience for freshly excited children. Kirsty and Stephanie refilled their mugs and resumed their serious conversation. A huddled, often muffled chat, dismembering

Stephanie's marriage; getting into the demands and distribution of what was once the essence of the Gayle partnership. Stephanie lying down, and Kirsty resting on her elbows; it was like counselling. Craig Gayle's market business was a considerable money maker, and a job he relished. His alcohol intake was just as sizable, and Stephanie was determined she was jumping ship and heading for a divorce. A determination to keep the house, achieve a maintenance agreement to cover her social needs and the needs of the children. The 'bastard' could manage all that, and throw in a decent car. There would be more days like this. Stephanie was gathering steam and she spoke through gritted teeth. Kirsty was seeing the anger. Squirming a little as her dear friend was nearing a rant. She stroked Stephanie's arm and offered a knowing smile. She was sympathetic, almost empathetic.

Stephanie paused, realising she was tackling an uncomfortable truth, perhaps spoiling their idyllic afternoon. She smiled to herself, a broader one to Kirsty. There were shouts from high branches as the children boasted their climbing success. Both mothers applauded and hollered their advice on safety, eventually tempting the mountaineers down from their perches with caramel-coated ice cream.

Afternoons like this one float randomly as a cloud. Stephanie and Kirsty lay back in a dreamy sun and the flickering shadows of overhanging branches. Children nattered and ran, scampered and crawled, entertaining themselves. The women spoke on. Now warm and connecting, understanding and bonding.

Kirsty was, with all senses, reliving that day. In the cold street, feeling the consoling sun, the slight coarseness of the blanket on her back, a cacophony of excited children's voices, tasting the fruitiness of the cool wine, watching Stephanie's breathing frame in her pink dress; rising and lowering as if she was showcasing being alive. Kirsty heard the singing of her reassuring expressions, the warmth of her living body. But as much as Kirsty tried, she couldn't hold on to her reverie. Reality and the sordid present replaced the perfection of her memory. She scuttled home, trying to retain a slice of her vision.

Chapter Three

Kirsty plucked the children from a waiting bunch swarming and chirping at the school gates. They were herded into the car. She didn't look at anyone else. But several parents looked knowingly at her.

'Charlie's pinching me,' Justine moaned. A day at school had helped her forget her mother's dark mood that morning.

'Not!' Charlie responded, as he shuffled along the back seat to reach his sister.

'Mum?' pleaded Justine.

'Cut it out. I'm not in the mood,' Kirsty managed.

Elliot sat at the front, his seat when his father wasn't there. His head into a book. Nothing much rattled him. Took after his dad, according to Kirsty.

Conversation at the minimum, the children rushed into the house and headed for their rooms. Each with their own mission. Elliot to sit at his orderly desk and press on with a few tasks set at school. Justine to search a cupboard for a skirt someone was on about at lunchtime, and Charlie grappling with an old electronic game that had defeated him before breakfast.

Evening descended quickly. Autumn was a rat for curling up the day. A miserable dank evening. Kirsty was edgy and not looking forward to the subterfuge of night. He would be back. Skulking around the house, scaring the shit out of her.

'What's this?' questioned Justine examining her dinner plate.

'Eat it.' Kirsty wasn't in the mood for our Miss Fussy tonight.

'Is it carbohydrate?' Justine retorted.

'It's pasta. Out of a packet, if the cardboard in the waste bin is anything to go by,' Elliot smartly informed everyone.

'Just a quick one tonight. It's been a busy day,' Kirsty explained, dishing up some sugary mush out of a can for dessert.

'Well, I like it,' Charlie mumbled, spluttering some of the pale sauce across the table.

A meal that wasn't a success. Justine didn't succeed in consuming much, despite her thorough inspection. Elliot and Charlie cleaned their plates, but they always did. No compliments were offered to the chef. Kirsty only went through the motions and wasn't out to produce a culinary masterpiece. Her mind was elsewhere.

Gradually and with an increasing degree of concern, the children were bedded down. Kirsty had the empty, exposed ground floor to herself. Room after room of corners and alcoves. Darker and perilous. She had always prided herself on the openness of the house. Free and uninhibited. But now the curtains were essential; drawn to keep out the prying gloom and those who conspired at that time. Once again, Kirsty was in her fortress. Once again, her faith was in the wine glass. She waited.

Astonished by the apparent conspicuousness, the doorbell rang. It was a diabolical noise. Some tune that Tom had insisted on; could be heard in the garden. Surely Craig Gayle wasn't now coming to the front entrance? Kirsty edged to the spyhole in the heavy door. Shifting warily. It was a young person, male.

With the same hospitality she proffered to the Jehovah

Witnesses, Kirsty opened the door; just a conversation crack awarded to unwelcomed callers.

'Hi.' A weak and strangled greeting from the gangling youth trying to peer through the measly gap.

Kirsty had to pull the door open that bit further. 'Hello.' The sound of recognition and surprise. Wrestling between cordiality and caution, she paused. And then, almost choking on her words, she carried on. 'Come in. Yes, you should come in.'

Displaying the awkwardness of a trainee usherette, Kirsty guided her visitor to the lounge. A room that Tom insisted, to her fury, on calling the sitting room. Dressed in the uniform of his age, sagging jeans, unimpressive top and Converse trainers, he plonked down on one of the sofas. Seventeen years old, Kirsty hadn't seen Nicholas Gayle for a long time. Now he was a lanky young man and no longer the kid on the first rung of adolescence when his mother, Stephanie, had disappeared.

'Been a long time,' Kirsty muttered.

'Sorry,' came the uneasy reply. Nicholas's eyes swung round the room, surveying his new environment. He'd been there before, but he needed time to readjust and remember. 'Not sure why. Things have been difficult.' He was attempting to channel his thoughts and master his words.

'So what's the reason for the visit?' Kirsty was helping the flummoxing youngster.

'There comes a time,' Nicholas began – it sounded like a string of clichés would spill out – 'when you get things in perspective, and your head seems to sort them out. A sort of clarity where there was a thick mist you couldn't see through. Am I making any sense?' His wide eyes questioned Kirsty.

'Keep going. It's fine.' Kirsty hadn't the foggiest, but her face appeared to show an understanding.

'When Mum went missing, I lost my way. Nothing seemed real. The other kids and I thought she'd stormed off and would be back. For a long time, I truly believed she'd come cheerfully through the front door. I was fooling myself. We all were.' Nicholas sunk a little. 'But now I can put things in their place, and I'm not sure I like what I'm seeing.'

Kirsty felt like cuddling him but fought off that instinct. Nicholas was the eldest Gayle child. Not Craig's. Stephanie had survived a short, brutal first marriage and escaped with one boy, Nicholas. He had become a fully accepted part of the new unit, especially as Stephanie had produced four others in quick succession with Craig. In the beginning, it was Nicholas that Kirsty had hoped would be the leading player in the hunt for his mother.

'What are you seeing?' Kirsty urged.

'I understand so much more. The day Mum went and all that had happened before, and all that I should have been aware of after. As though it's fitting into place. A completed puzzle. That's no longer a puzzle. I've solved it. I think. Don't like it… don't like it at all.' Nicholas squeezed his lips tightly.

'What have you solved, Nicholas?' Kirsty quizzed, refreshed by what she was hearing.

'Things at home weren't good. I'd blocked out most of that. You do. Try and keep up the pretence of the happy family. At that time, it was a very gloomy place. Perhaps you respected other people's loss. You're really still a kid, and the others were very young. Dad seemed to be suffering. Possibly didn't get my head round it at the time.'

'Of course, we were all in shock and confusion. I know I was completely derailed. Keep going.' Kirsty urged Nicholas on.

'Most evenings when I arrived home from school at that time, there were rows. Now I recall how awful they were. Both accusing the other. Other men and stuff. And violence. And, of course, money. He never liked parting with his "hard-earned" fucking money. I had definitely shut that out for a long time. Dad would beat Mum. There were times she had gone to the doctor's and even the hospital with her injuries. Arms black and blue; maybe elsewhere.' A spike of anger in his voice.

'You know Mum asked him for a divorce, don't you?' Nicholas's eyes were damp now.

'Yes, I knew.'

'Did you know she was due to see her solicitor the very next day?' Nicholas asked. 'The very next day after she left us.' His head sunk to his chest.

'Yes.' Kirsty's head followed, indicating a knowing, accommodating listener.

Nicholas reached a second breath. 'All this week, since I've been rebuilding that time, I've looked. Searched the Internet to remind me. There were notes at that time; my dad's notes that the police found. In his writing; a note found in his briefcase about disposing of a body, a human body. My mum's human body? At sea, by fire, acid, a landfill site; it was all there. And in the three days before he was in touch with the police, there was his large white van from the fruit and veg business in the drive. He would never usually bring that home.'

Kirsty nodded her knowledge of these things.

'And taking nothing with her, she just vanished. And the police sat on their Metropolitan arses. Of course, they questioned him and asked us kids a volley of relevant stuff, but it all went quiet, went flat.' Nicholas sighed. He seemed resigned.

'We are really raking up the past here. I'm sorry to say the only thing this will do is tear you all apart. The whole matter is an emotional cul-de-sac, and I know, Nicholas dear.' Kirsty bent forward and laid a hand on his tilted head. 'Coffee?' She thought a while and was aware he was nearly old enough now. 'Or something a little stronger?'

'Coffee's fine.' He was tempted but felt he had to maintain a clear head.

'Coming up.' Kirsty scuttled off to the kitchen. And while she stood by the grumbling kettle, she lifted the window blind to peer into the blackness of the night, and wondered if she was going to get a visitor. This time there was even more at risk. Could Craig Gayle come creeping into her garden while his stepson poured out the dirt in her lounge, while Nicholas condemned the murderer who was slinking around, determined to haunt her?

'It's hot, careful.' Kirsty handed over a mug of steaming coffee and headed back for her essential large glass of Cabernet Sauvignon.

Nicholas held the mug with both hands, blew at the liquid and took short slurps. And between tackling his beverage, he divulged to Kirsty what had made him leave the solidarity of the Gayle household and come over to the tormenting woman, his mother's dear friend, that his stepfather constantly ranted about.

'Dad came home last week with this Portuguese guy, Demetrio, who, he said, had started work at his firm and needed lodgings until he found something. We didn't think much about it. He was moderately pleasant, if a little odd.' Nicholas took another sip and gulped heavily. 'And then yesterday, I came home from college early. Inset day, I think they call it. Well, we all got let out after lunch. I suppose I didn't make much noise, and the other kids, being at their school, weren't coming home.' Now Nicholas was breathing heavier, labouring.

'You okay?' Kirsty enquired, somewhat concerned.

'Yeah, I'll be fine. Well, I stood in the hallway laying down my schoolbag and stuff. And there was this noise from upstairs.' Nicholas sucked in through his teeth. Kirsty leaned forward. 'Groaning and thumping, and smothered talking. Sort of stuff I'd heard when Mum and Dad were first together, but different. For an instance, I thought my mother was back. Hoping. But it had been too long. He'd got another woman. He was at home having sex with a new tart in his life. It was a bit of a blow. I suppose I was distressed that he would be doing that with a replacement for Mum. I stole up to my room, trying to keep my distance from the humping sounds still coming from his bedroom. It nearly took my head off. I couldn't believe what I was hearing. I had to edge closer to his door. I listened. Warm voices. The voices of two men, yes, two men. My dad and that bloke. He and his Portuguese lodger were in bed together. Now they were whispering like... like... like lovers.' Nicholas screwed up his face and gave out short explosions of choking. 'It was sickening. I darted downstairs, scooped up my bag, opened and slammed the front door and scampered back to my room and kept quiet. Don't think they suspected or knew what I'd heard.' He searched Kirsty's face for some response.

'Bloody hell,' Kirsty mumbled softly. 'Now that's blown me away. No idea. Where do we go from here?'

Nicholas stood as if he'd committed treachery, about to turn and run. Kirsty grabbed him as he lurched towards the door. A mother's hug. A cuddle of comfort. She would hold him till he was composed enough to leave.

Chapter Four

Over the next four days, Kirsty went through the motions. Husband Tom would be home in a week and staying for three. The children were managing, even if their mother was wandering around a little dozy, yet mellow, deep in thought. She hadn't had an evening visitor recently, and her picketing of the Gayle home had been only occasional. Stuck outside the Gayle house, she was experiencing different feelings now that the picture inside was so changed. Nicholas had phoned once to apologise and plead secrecy.

Sat over a morning tea, house evacuated, about ten, the ringing phone broke her reverie. Unsure whether she would answer it, she listened to the drilling chime until her own voice interrupted and told the caller she was out or unavailable. It was one of those answer machines where you could hear the message being delivered. No one she knew; a low, unsure and broken voice leaving his number and requesting a call back. Kirsty was far from concerned and dunked another biscuit in the tea.

Eventually, the flashing red light on the answering device that dogged her movements about the house was annoying enough for her to listen to the message again. Who was he, and what did he want? Probably of no importance and not demanding her attention, she rubbed it off her mental catalogue of essential things to do that day. Not much; a short list.

Following an unremarkable day where she prepared a little

for Tom's return and reeled through some pages of cheap dresses on her iPad, Kirsty routinely picked up the children in her normal snatch-and-grab manner. A journey home where there was more shuffling and bag searching than there was conversation, a tumbling from the car and scampering kids off to their bases.

In the void between school run and evening meal, Kirsty played the message that was still clogging up the memory on her answer machine. Along with some funny ones and the eerie voice of an uncle who had died; strangely kept. Kirsty grabbed a pad and pen. She jotted down the number. And with nothing else to do, rang it. After four rings, a recorded message informed her that 'Bairstow and Brothers is now closed. Leave a message and we'll call you back, or call again. Working hours are four a.m. till twelve thirty p.m. Thank you'.

Times were when you'd sit there wondering, baffled by the mysterious firm that you had been contacted by. Now, of course, a simple search on her tablet would reveal all. Although there was no website, it was easy to locate the business using various sites. Bairstow and Brothers were suppliers of exotic fruits and vegetables and operated from the New Covent Garden. Kirsty momentarily, and quite without thinking, dismissed the call as she had never had dealings with these people and bought all her produce locally. A wrong number. It was clear that the opening times reflected the nature of their company. Like a grenade had gone off. Idiot! She was certainly not alert today. Fruit and vegetables, New Covent Garden. That's where Craig Gayle was based, where he made all his precious money.

Now her sleep would be dogged by speculation. And she knew she was heading for a really bad day if she didn't get a decent amount of shuteye. It was a night for some assistance. She popped in a couple of melatonin pills between the last glug of wine and her ablutions.

Groggy and bedraggled. Kirsty was a mess in the morning. Children, quite used to such things, muddled through. After a faltering school delivery and a couple of coffees, it had to be the phone. A young female, plastic Cockney, probably Essex. 'Bairstow and Bruvvers. Can I 'elp?'

Kirsty thought she was able to speak coherently, but out spluttered a gob full of nonsense. 'Sorry,' she managed, taking control. 'Had a call yesterday, from your number, a man. He asked me to call back.'

'Name?' A single snapped word from the girl.

'Didn't leave a name. Just a call. That's what he said.' Kirsty faded.

'What's yer name, love? I'll ask the fellas. Don't mind the bloody silly music when I put you on 'old.' More human now, our Essex lass.

And she was right; the music stuttered and hissed, crackled and sizzled. ''ello.' Abruptly the broken tune was replaced by a hoarse male voice. Most probably the voice that left the initial message. It was difficult to hear him clearly. He was in a working environment; other people, heavy movements, crates scraping and the exchange of banter. 'Is that Kirsty?'

'Yes.' Kirsty was barely audible herself.

'Look, I can't talk now. But I need to. I'll call you back when the panic's over 'ere, and there are fewer ears. Name's Steve. About two?' A rough diamond. Naturally involved at his end, yet somewhat cautious.

'Two's okay.' Kirsty was thinking of more to say, but Steve had slapped down the receiver his end.

Intrigue rather than concern dominated the space between her words with Steve, the New Covent Garden fruit and veg man, and his call back. Had she made this more of a curiosity than it was? Wasn't it probably only a matter of produce promotion? A harmless contact?

Just past two. Three minutes and seven seconds, she had timed it, the phone's shrill din erupted beneath her waiting hand. 'Yes?'

'Steve Bairstow.' A long pause. 'I suppose you're wondering why I called?'

'Yes.' Kirsty's reply continued the economy of words.

'Well, what I need to say ain't right for the phone. I want to speak to you face to face.' Kirsty felt reluctance in his voice.

'Where? What about?' Kirsty was getting jittery. 'I don't know you. Out of the blue you ring me up. I do need to know more.'

'Look, I ain't playing no games. This is something that is up your alley. You'll be interested. A lot of people will be interested.' Steve was a little rattled.

'Give me a clue. I do need something to convince me that this isn't a load of tosh. Meeting total strangers is not a usual pastime.' Kirsty was pushing the fruit and veg man. A grubby man who still fingered the harshly folded and heavily stained flyer that Kirsty had distributed among the market tribesmen.

'Right. This is as far as I'm going. You came looking at the market at the time. Concerns that shit Craig Gayle and 'is missing wife. 'ave I said enough?'

He had. Kirsty flopped; almost dropped the phone. 'Okay. I'll meet you. Where? When?' She didn't need any further convincing.

Steve went quiet, as though thinking. 'Not sure of your

area. Name somewhere. I can look it up.'

Kirsty shook her head. Clandestine meetings weren't easy to make decisions about on the spot. She knew it had to be safe, where there were people. In the back of her mind she had all manner of scenarios tumbling about. Kidnapping, rape, the lot. 'There's a pub cum wine bar in Esher, The Bear,' she croaked.

'Esher?' It was as if she had said Mars. 'Where's that? No, don't worry, I'll look it up. Day, time?' Steve's grip was sweaty. He had spoken long enough.

'Tomorrow night. Eight; okay?' Kirsty replied as smartly as she could.

'Eight at the... The Bear. Wear a scarf or something. We don't want no mix-ups.'

'A red one. See you then.' Kirsty expelled a long flow of air. She was glad that was over; not at all happy about this rendezvous.

Kirsty's mind was a cocktail of assorted consequences throughout the day. Most domestic activities were robotic, lacking intention or involvement. Frantic calls to friends she hadn't kept close were treated with suspicion until she found a parent from Justine's class who would sit in for the evening. It was the one who most people avoided as she would 'talk the hind legs off a donkey', whatever that meant. Kirsty was aware many parents made deliberate efforts to circumnavigate her. It took some rather compelling lying to squeeze herself out the door away from the woman's rambling blather. Kirsty pitied her poor children left to face this woman's rattling voice.

Esher's erstwhile business community was on its last round after sliding out of local estate agencies and independent financial advice offices. The younger ones with only a mother to go home to. There would be a slight break before the more serious drinkers arrived, those who knew the manager, knew the best ales, knew where they always sat, knew who was a stranger.

The Bear was a spruced-up provincial pub that now preferred to be known as just a bar. Kirsty wasn't too keen on the stench of stale beer that seemed to live in the carpet. She studied the people. Still clustered in grubby conversation were the soon-to-leave, just-about-had-enough, spiv office community. What appeared to be a student was huddled over his laptop using the 'free Wi-Fi for all our customers' and a few couples in corners that Kirsty mischievously thought were involved in surreptitious affairs. No Steve. She ordered a small Pinot Grigio; something harmless, but something to hold. She sat conspicuously, fiddled with wispy tassels of the red scarf.

Without intention you picture a person from their voice. And without exception you get it wrong. Steve Bairstow was not at all like Kirsty's mental picture she had taken with her to this meeting. Small, middle-aged, slightly bent-over, scant hair and keen not to stand out. A sheepish man of the market community, shuffling round barrows and barrowmen, wads of cash, a ready joke, out for a bargain, dealing and dispatching. He hovered between the barman ready to serve, a carved smile on his face, and the red scarf he was there to meet. Fumbling in his pockets, beyond the grimy flyer still stuffed firmly down that had led him there, he hastily ordered a small beer, bottle only.

'Kirsty?' his thick voice muttered as he approached her table.

'Yes. You Steve?'

Steve nodded and pulled out a chair. Some awkward smiles followed before they properly spoke. Not an easy conversation.

'So?' Kirsty offered, unsure of this shady character.

'Not used to this. Not my game normally.' Steve's eyes flickered, and he studied the few customers in the corners of the pub. He breathed heavily. 'Look, it's Craig Gayle. Been messing things up. I think it's time to tell someone.'

'Tell someone what?' Kirsty quizzed.

'A number of years ago, yeah 'bout that time, when 'is wife went missing. You know, all that fuss about 'er vanishing like. You waltzing round the stalls with leaflets and desperately searching.' Steve was quickly getting to the point.

'Yes. That was the disappearance of Stephanie, a great friend,' Kirsty earnestly declared. A school ma'am putting him right.

'Well, at that time us market lot were right be'ind Craig. There's a solidarity with us boys. Cops came round after you was there, but they was only asking about 'is movements and if we knew about 'is relationship wiv 'is missus. It were pretty basic stuff. No real investigation. You'd 'ave thought they'd 'ave done more.'

Kirsty was well aware of the background and the lack of police determination. 'I know,' she added, in an effort to not only assure him but to hopefully move it on.

'This is 'urting a bit.' Steve moved slightly closer to Kirsty, nearer to her ear. 'Craig Gayle, about that time, asked me about the shredder.'

'Shredder?' Kirsty asked, screwing up her nose.

'Call it a shredder, but nicknamed the Mangler. At Bairstow and Bruvvers, we trash all of the market waste. Sometimes there's massive wooden crates full of veg and stuff that won't sell or a duff lot that New Covent Garden can't lose. We get rid of all that, no matter what size or what material. We crush for England.' Steve was really loosening up. Almost selling the service. 'And best of all, we knows where to incinerate or dump it.'

'What did he ask you about?' Kirsty was getting the drift.

'Wanted to borrow it. The 'ole machinery over the weekend when we weren't there. Said 'e 'ad things to crush. A large load of watermelons or something that needed to go before it stank the place out. Asked 'ow much and stuff 'bout the sealed bins the mush went into.'

Deep in her stomach, a nagging nausea. She did her best to wipe away an unspeakable image of her beautiful friend being chopped to shreds, pulverised and despatched. 'Did you let him?' Kirsty managed.

'Well, no. I told 'im it would cost a thousand quid and 'e would need someone to show 'im 'ow to use it. Couldn't do it on 'is own.' Steve assured her.

'Didn't you think it strange? Wasn't it something you should have told the police at the time?' Kirsty was a little agitated. 'A woman goes missing, and her husband asks to use a machine that shreds anything and could be dumped anywhere? Surely you were suspicious; surely this was vital at that time?'

'As I said, in the market, there's an unwritten, unsaid agreement. We don't grass up our own. Solid as a rock we are.' A mixture of pride and apology.

'If this had come to light, the police would have nailed him.' Kirsty peered into her drink, crestfallen. 'So, why now? Why, after all this time, have you decided to tell… to tell me?'

'Not proud of it, but there's been some changes. Me and Craig 'ave some differences.' Steve became edgy.

'Changes? Differences?' Kirsty was feeling some rising anger. 'My beautiful friend, Stephanie, deserves more than this.'

Steve seemed to bend over further, and his speech thinner. 'We ain't all the same. I thought I was the only one at the market. Way I felt. You don't tell mates. Not in that place. So you keep it to yourself. Pretence and bravado.' Steve was struggling with this. 'We occasionally need extra 'elp in the market when it gets busy. Specially after 'arvest time and when the ships come in with produce. Well, this guy from Portugal arrived. Good worker. 'Andsome bloke. Stood out. Used to watch 'im working. Tight, muscular build. Tanned. Mass of black 'air.' Steve had a picture in his head that he was surveying. 'Look, Kirsty. I'm gay. A fucking queer. All right?' It was as if he'd dumped it and was spreading his whole life on the table.

'Doesn't worry me. We live in a more understanding world now; people don't care.' Kirsty did her best to comfort him.

'Market ain't your understanding world. It's where everyone's straight. Benders ain't tolerated. Get the stick, get chased out. You'll never change 'em. Might seem brutal, but it's a fact. So you play the game, and 'opefully they think you're as narrow-minded as them; even throw in some abuse about 'omos.' Steve blew out some air.

'Well, it turned out that Demetrio, the Portuguese Adonis, was on my wavelength. It didn't take long before we went for a casual drink, drank too much and slipped back to my place. It was sweet. Kept it quiet. He was just what I needed.' Steve was having pictures.

Kirsty was hearing things that weren't part of her agenda. 'I'll get another drink,' she offered. It would break his distraction and perhaps get him back on her track.

She was soon back with a repeat order and some nuts. 'You

were telling me about the changes,' she encouraged.

Steve sat back. 'Together for about six months, perfect, me and Demetrio. Then that fucking Craig Gayle destroys everything. Thought 'e was as straight as a ruler; married with kids. Always the big bloke about the market. Never an 'int 'e would be interested. Bought Demetrio stuff. Took 'im places. Wormed 'is way in. Sure Demetrio and I 'ad some time together, but I sensed 'e wasn't the same.' Steve drifted off again.

'And?' Kirsty urged.

'After I learn 'e's playing around with Gayle. My Demetrio and that bastard. Was I sick? Couldn't show it at work, but I felt like doing meself in. Lost everything.'

Kirsty felt like moving across and giving Steve Bairstow some succour. She resisted. 'So our Craig Gayle bats for both sides, and he's stolen your Portuguese partner.' Kirsty sounded very matter-of-fact, even to herself. 'Sorry.' Hardly sincere.

'Still steaming. Still ranting when I'm alone.' Steve rocked in his chair.

Kirsty made her move. 'What's needed, Steve, is for Craig Gayle to pay for this; for your pain and for poor Stephanie.' She lowered herself, almost talking at table-top level to the market man who was hunched over. 'Are you willing to tell the police this? Are you brave enough to repeat what you've told me in court?' Kirsty held her breath.

'I 'spose I'm a broken man. Can't see much point in things staying as they are. Won't go back to the market. Me bruvvers will run the business. I want out. Yeah, I want to see that shit Gayle suffer. I'll talk. Probably do me good. Flush out some demons. Yeah.' Steve lifted his head and exhaled audibly.

Like a hunter with her prey held safely in a cage, Kirsty

began some hard-nosed formalities. She took down Steve's address and mobile number; assured him that contact would be safe, and in a motherly fashion, explained what she was going to do. Steve shrugged and fidgeted. He needed to get home. Without much more than a brief holding of hands, both hands, and a purposeful squeeze, they went their separate ways.

There was still time when Kirsty arrived home and had shunted the warbling babysitter out the door.

'Hello. I'm not sure who I exactly need to speak to, but I want to discuss a matter concerning the unsolved disappearance of Stephanie Gayle.' Kirsty spoke to an anonymous civilian police worker at a call centre that now took messages from the public. Voices of little interest and doubtful concern.

'Please leave a contact number, and an officer will return your call,' came the response.

Kirsty confirmed all details. She now began to arrange a strategy in her head.

Chapter Five

Detective Inspector Warren Yates hadn't moved much and wasn't moving anywhere. He was a DI, and that's where he was staying. He'd witnessed colleagues shoot past him in the promotion lottery, but he knew he would always have the wrong numbers. Should have joined the Masons, should have solved more high-profile crimes, should have sucked up to some large egos in the Met. But never did. Still, there were only six years until he could retire.

Warren's desk was an old rocky oak one, handed down from the super's office. It sat before a semi-circular window on the top floor of a dusty annexe neighbouring the Wimbledon nick. He wasn't alone. This was where nothing much happened; where paperwork that had been through all the departments, and where processes finally came to rest. DI Yates was in charge, he smiled at that, of Cold Cases, usually murder. Some so cold they were frozen. Abandoned 1960s corpses where a killer was never found, and was probably dead themselves by now.

A Wednesday morning. A few nagging files that had to sit nearby as there was the chance of a fresh examination, and not much else except Warren's well-sharpened pencil, his reading glasses and a begging space for the next assignment. He needed some excitement in his dreary life. He knew he was a damn good copper; trouble was they, those that were regaled and worming their way to the top, thought he was 'too old school' and 'rough-edged'. Warren couldn't care a toss.

'There you go, Sherlock.' A feisty young female dumped a limp beige folder into the inspector's waiting space between pencil and spectacles. Warren watched her ample, yet not unpleasant, bottom sashay in and out of other supposedly-active desks and disappear to more productive parts of the building.

He read the cover. *Stephanie Gayle* scribbled large, followed by a date. Four years old; recent in his book. Attached at the corner was stuck a yellow note giving the details of Kirsty's call. Warren wasn't going to phone until he had some idea of the case. He read through the history of a scant police investigation, of the arrest of Craig Gayle, incriminating notes, of the delay in reporting Stephanie missing, her vanishing without the stuff that fleeing people take with them, some brief investigation at the market and the volatile relationship with Stephanie. No trace, no body. Not enough evidence to proceed. Warren closed the file. For now.

Over a coffee in the rattling canteen, he seemed to recall some details of the vanishing mother from East Molesey. A cigarette, only the one and he was definitely going to quit, huddled outside with another ostracised smoker helped him remember more. And by the time he had returned to his neat desk and the dog-eared folder, aspects of the enquiry were coming to the surface. Warren read through what little information there was again. He grabbed the phone.

Kirsty had been sitting by, or very near, her telephone. 'Hello.' She hoped it was the police, but she displayed none of her anxiousness just in case it was an unrelated, random call.

'Detective Inspector Yates, Metropolitan Police.' Warren made his opening sound grander and his rank more impressive. There was something 1990s about his delivery. 'Understand you rang in, Mrs Foster? A call yesterday concerning a past investigation by this force?'

'Yes, about... Stephanie Gayle.' Kirsty's voice croaked and broke a little.

'Is this something important, something that you wish to talk about on the telephone?' the policeman quizzed.

Of course Kirsty's phone wasn't bugged, and there were no hidden microphones in the house, but with the hounding she had suffered, none of this was certain. She wasn't sure what to do.

'I say, you still there Mrs Foster?' Warren asked.

'Sorry. I suppose this is a matter where I should talk to you in person.' Kirsty didn't sound that confident in what she was saying. Still unsure about a phantom listener, she continued. 'Could I come and see you?'

From sounding the influential policeman, DI Yates felt his pretentions sliding away. His humble desk in the attic of an annexe. His lowly position in a room full of clerks. But there was a saving grace; a designated interview room in the proper station next door he could use. 'Wimbledon Police Station; do you know it?'

'I'll get there. Look it up and use my satnav,' Kirsty assured him.

'Tomorrow at three?' Warren knew the times when the lepers from next door could use it.

'Fine.'

'Ask for Detective Inspector Yates at the front desk. See you at three.' Warren was back to sounding important.

After a day collating stuff in her head and with children collection covered, Kirsty drove up a cluttered A3 to Wimbledon. The police station was near the town centre, and there was plenty of parking in the shopping centre nearby.

'Detective Yates?' Kirsty requested at the reception. She didn't realise she was dropping important details. Warren needed to hold on to the inspector. Give a man some dignity.

'Yates?' The sergeant on duty puzzled. An officer far away, burdened with hapless enquiries, wasn't easy to place. He turned to a colleague. 'Yates?'

'Top floor, next door,' he was informed.

'Take a seat, ma'am. I'll just ring through.' Polite yet intrigued.

Warren was down like a shot. He'd been ready all day. Nothing much else was happening. He ushered Kirsty into a small room uncomfortably heated by a huge old radiator, just like the ones she'd had at school.

The inspector plonked the Gayle file on a bare wooden table and gestured for Kirsty to sit. He even offered a bobby's smile. You know, one that fills the face but is far from genuine. 'I'm all ears.' Warren sat deeply in his chair and invited Kirsty to outline the new information.

'Well.' Kirsty caught her breath. 'As you know, my good friend Stephanie Gayle simply disappeared some four years ago.' Kirsty looked over at the scruffy folder central on the desk. 'I see you've got the details. At the time, and which I strongly believe, her husband, Craig, was the prime suspect. He was arrested and questioned about her disappearance. The police trod water and did nothing. Even though there was evidence he intended to harm her, kill her, there were no charges. He walked away scot-free.' Kirsty was heating up.

'It was all stacked against him. Notes on how to dispose of a body. Didn't report her missing for three days. His van at home. On the edge of divorce. Beatings and rows. His love of money and fear of her getting some. It all added up. But you, well, the police, wore blinkers. There was no real investigation. They didn't even interview me.' Kirsty was waving her hands now.

This was unsettling Warren Yates. He was used to a placid environment. This woman was erupting. 'Hold on Mrs Foster, not so fast.'

Warren opened the file. 'Tea?'

'Please.' Kirsty hadn't finished, only on pause.

Tea arrived on a metal tray alongside a meagre plate of crumbling digestives. DI Yates flicked papers as Kirsty sipped from her cup.

'No body,' he muttered, still poring over the notes. 'No forensics.' A further stifled utterance. 'Without some real evidence; when it's all circumstantial, you're stumped. The CPS won't consider taking this all the way when you're relying on assumptions.' Warren looked up into Kirsty's glazed eyes. 'So what have you got to offer? Are you hoping we can get this off the ground?'

'Fresh start,' Kirsty began. 'And yes, I am hoping to kick you into action. First, I have at least one new witness, maybe two, and if you include me, three. Also fresh evidence and motive.'

'You've got me interested.' Warren would love it if he was seen to be successfully reviving a defunct case.

For the next twenty minutes, Kirsty fuelled the now attentive police officer with the account given by Nicholas Gayle and the proposal made to Steve Bairstow. Warren scribbled in his policeman's pad, flipping leaves with vigour as the tales unfolded. He spoke rarely. Pausing Kirsty only when his pencil needed sharpening or she spoke too quickly. Other officers occasionally poked their heads round the door. No one expected a tired old inspector from Cold Cases to monopolise the interview room.

When she had finished, or the relevance terminated for him, Warren Yates sat back in his chair, desperate for a fag. A long, deeply inhaled cloud of smoke. His face flashed pleasure. Both from the thought of the cigarette and the realisation that these new leads could spring this case open. 'It would be unkind not to say I am pleased,' he announced. 'From what you've told me, I'm sure we can move forward.' It was a copper's way of telling Kirsty that what she had told him wasn't being binned, that it was solid, usable information that he hoped would be pursued.

'Are we looking at a new investigation?' eagerly queried Kirsty.

'Early days. I need to talk to both of these characters. If they support all you've told me, then we are, subject to the okay from some rather awkward gentlemen in this building, definitely re-examining the viability of this matter. I can say no more.' Warren was inwardly dreaming ahead.

'Great.' Kirsty breathed out heavily.

'I will need particulars here. All addresses and telephone numbers. Let's hope no one changes their story now that Plod is asking the questions. I'll be in touch.' DI Yates held Kirsty's hand, grinned respectfully, winked and wished her a safe journey and bright future.

When Detective Inspector Yates skipped through the drudge of an office to the sanctuary of his wobbly old oak desk, his face radiated satisfaction. The other clerical drones, motionless and bewildered. Now he really was on a mission.

Nothing is easy. In order to interview Nicholas Gayle, Warren had to prise him from the family home on a pretext, and was only allowed to talk to Nicholas with a social worker present. His version confirmed Kirsty's account. Steve Bairstow was difficult to nail down. After a few false starts, Warren cornered him. An identical explanation with a little more detail of the grinding, incineration and deposition of waste. Some sordid accounts of homosexual behaviour that had him grimacing. However, he would certainly speak out publicly. Warren rubbed his hands gleefully.

Now for the difficult part.

'You want to do what?' Chief Superintendent Collins-Maynard exclaimed. 'We've shelved that one once. You want to unwrap a case that we've satisfactorily stored without much fuss and acrimony? Have you any idea of the money involved? We are supposed to be cutting back. Watching our fucking pennies. And here you are proposing to begin a multi-staffed operation that will cost tens, maybe hundreds of thousands. Shit.'

'Ticks all the boxes. It's all laid down. If new and reliable evidence is obtained that will most likely lead to a successful prosecution, it must be followed. That's why I'm sitting daily at my desk wading through these obsolete enquiries. Not often do I find a damn good reason to reopen a case. This is one.' Warren was enjoying his moment in front of the man who had helped send him to a crummy backwater in the annexe.

'I want all you have. Every dotted i and crossed t. No holes. No ambushes. The original file and every scrap of new material on my desk. And it had better be watertight. I won't let this pass until I am one hundred per cent.' Collins-Maynard growled. He was not a happy man.

Chapter Six

Tom Foster was back from the bastion oilfield in Nigeria. Kirsty was back to being a wife and mother. She could act differently now she wasn't in sole charge. Tom loved dealing with the kids and school. It gave her space. There wouldn't be any night time visits by Craig Gayle, and she wouldn't be sentinel outside his house. It would be sexist to admit a man made that difference; but it did.

Detective Inspector Yates, Cold Cases, phoned when Tom was stacking the car with kids, happy to be taken to school by the freshly arrived Dad they could show off to their classmates. A babble of noise. Kirsty was able to pick up the phone and still wave the carload goodbye. It was great; she hadn't needed to dress. Creased and stretched pyjamas, lounging.

'It's with the old man now. He's reluctant, of course. Budgets and savings,' explained Warren.

'Surely he can recognise how everything's changed. We've tipped the balance, haven't we? There's a strong case.' Kirsty's frustration was evident.

'Look, I'm making all the arrangements for a positive response. We need to catch that arsehole Gayle on the hop. Hopefully, he's unaware that the tables have turned.' Warren tried his best to bolster her.

'Keep in touch.' Kirsty could do nothing further. She would enjoy Tom being home and relish the whole family thing. Three weeks would fly by. It would be Easter before he was home again.

Evenings when the children had been tucked up, and their absent father couldn't escape without a tale about the desert and life in Africa, they spoke. No, they confided and shared admissions. If it weren't for the money, he would be at home commuting to a city desk and being a homely bloke in the stockbroker belt. She would have the security to meet more people, join a Pilates group and mingle with many more social grazers for lunch. Perhaps she would be able to put Craig Gayle to the bottom of her schedule or even caged a long way away.

Homecomings were much the same. There had been the obligatory sex; that was now a formality, almost a ritual. Living apart makes you a little selfish, and when you return you are forced to share your bubble. There are strains on a relationship. Tom and Kirsty shared their news and plans. Inevitably the subject rounded on the Gayles. How was she coping? Was she still parading outside his house? Wasn't it time to get over it, move on? Tom was only too aware of the obsession that gripped his wife and the toll it was taking. He was a touch jealous of Kirsty's relationship with Stephanie. She had always looked after herself and been a vivacious, optimistic, attractive individual. Now, tired, not haggard, but heading that way, he thought. Not that he would dare say.

Kirsty updated her agnostic husband. She wouldn't mention the intimidation, the nightly bullying, the photos. Definitely not the photos. 'Nicholas has been over.'

'Nicholas? Nicholas Gayle? What's that all about?' Tom was confused. 'He's kept his head down since this began. Something wake him up?'

'Not sure exactly, but I think the spell Craig had over him has been broken. He was holding on to the security of home, other children and his dad.'

'Stepdad,' interjected Tom, as if to add fuel to this breakup.

Kirsty continued. 'At that age, he found it difficult to cope with the loss of his mother; clung on to those around him. Small sisters and an apparently grieving father, stepfather. Now he feels things have slotted into place. Plus… he's seen through his stepfather. Seen another, not very orthodox side.'

'And that is?' Tom was showing interest.

'Craig Gayle has someone else in his life,' Kirsty smugly declared.

'Well, it's been some time. Surely he's allowed to, dare I say it, move on?' A male understanding of the situation, or so he thought.

'Another man.' Kirsty dropped her bombshell.

'You're joking!' Tom snorted. 'Craig Gayle's turned queer? Is that boy sure?'

'Oh, yes. I'm sorry to say poor Nicholas heard them at it. Traumatising for a young man. I've had confirmation elsewhere. Our Mr Gayle has retreated into his true sexuality. No wonder he wanted to get rid of his wonderful wife; wanted her out of the way so he could shack up with some bloke.' Kirsty was becoming agitated.

Tom slid back down in the sofa, hand on chin, thoughtful. 'Wow, that's quite a shock. And you say you've proof?'

'As I was going on to say, there's more. Had a call from a guy who works at New Covent Garden, like Craig. Runs a waste disposal business there with his brothers. Seems Craig Gayle wanted access to his machinery at the time Steph went missing. Blurting it out now because it seems the mystery bedded lover-boy down the road was stolen goods. Belonged to this gay guy named Steve. He's willing to blow his anonymity and tell all to the police.' Kirsty précised.

It was a difficult bundle for Tom to take in. 'So, you are telling me that Gayle, our big man at the market, tried to hire the means to crush and dump a body from a company that disposes of vegetable trash? And the person concerned didn't tell anybody about this until now, four years later?'

'Exactly. Until Craig Gayle whisked away this guy's Portuguese rent boy, it's amazing how the scorned react. Well, I suppose it isn't.' Kirsty was empathising. 'This Steve was initially determined to maintain the silence of the market. They're like a tribe there. Now he's ditching the closet circle at New Covent Garden and broadcasting for all to hear.'

Tom was reeling. 'So, what's going to happen now? Hadn't you better tell someone?' Coming to terms with all the news had his head whirring.

'And that's another thing.' Kirsty was ready to detail her meeting with Warren Yates; a little discomfited by her mission. 'I've already taken this further; to the police.'

'What?' Now she was really surprising her husband.

'All this evidence is sitting in front of the officer in charge of cold, unsolved cases, and he's taking it to the top.' Kirsty leant to touch Tom on the knee. 'From Detective Inspector Yates' reaction, we might at last get some justice for... Stephanie.' Just the thought of her absent friend tugged at her throat; she almost choked.

*

In his clinical office, the décor a Spartan idea from the commissioner, Collins-Maynard flustered through the documents that his side-lined inspector had inconveniently thrust upon him. He was aggressively searching for an opt-out. The last thing he needed was a massive investigation that would involve unchartered man-hours and a bloody drain on resources. If possible, there were flaws that an experienced officer could discover. The chief superintendent was a man for detail and close examination. He was a man who had discarded his jacket, was perspiring visibly and working a lot fucking later than he wanted.

Pubs had closed, people had been contacted over their dinner, and only a skeleton staff remained at Wimbledon Police Station when a stooped Chief Superintendent Collins-Maynard scowled his way from the station and into a waiting black cab.

Chapter Seven

A heavy rhythmic whine, that appeared to smother all other noises, saturated the air and woke her. Kirsty shook the tousled mop of ragged hair that swung from her head. She straightened her rumpled pyjamas. Tom had left for the desert outback of Nigeria; she didn't need to look glamorous in bed. Anyway, it was winter wear. You only dressed for the season, at the call of the temperature.

From the window, she saw it, a circling helicopter; blue and white, quite low. And in the road, fierce drilling cars, flickering blue lights spraying the houses, no sirens. Following, vans, same lights, same silence. Justine wandered in, fists in her eye sockets, rubbing away sleep. 'What's happening?' she slurred.

'Police. Swarming the area.' Kirsty wiped some condensation from a window pane and screwed up her eyes. 'Not sure what they're doing.'

Everyone assembled for breakfast. Having been told about the cops outside, the boys dashed to the front room to search the neighbourhood for excitement. Not much to see, they wandered back. 'Robbery, eh?' Charlie suggested roguishly, bright-eyed for this time in the morning.

'Probably just some accident on the by-pass.' Kirsty tried to quell the interest as she delivered breakfast. Rethinking the chores and the timetable now that she was back in sole charge.

To the pure delight of both boys in particular, and Justine, when their chaos of a carload reached the corner where the Gayle family had their 1930s detached house, they saw the source of the activity. A scrum of police vehicles filled every kerb; lights still flashing. Officers in white overalls and boots milled purposefully around the driveway and between Craig Gayle's cars. Officers unreeling flapping barriers of yellow tape. A house under siege. Above, the swishing chopper hovered.

Kirsty was stuck, mouth open, eyes paralysed. Warren Yates hadn't called. Metropolitan Police in total shutdown without a word. An inner welling caught her, bubbling between shock and satisfaction.

It wasn't until early afternoon that official word arrived. Kirsty was thinking inside her coffee cup and flicking at the daily paper; more pictures and headlines than a real read. An apologetic knock at the door. Kirsty was quick to react, keen to glean information. She wasn't expecting a complete stranger; a black face.

'Mrs Foster?' A tight, well-practised voice. 'You are Kirsty Foster?'

'Yes, yes.' Her visitor recognised a familiar response.

'Sorry if I've startled you. My name is Detective Sergeant Leonard. I'm working on this case with Detective Inspector Yates, who I believe you've met. When I say this case, I mean the investigation into the disappearance of Stephanie Gayle.' Sergeant Leonard explained speedily. 'Inspector Yates wanted me to have a word. As you can see,' Leonard waved his arm to gesticulate up the road, 'we've arrived en masse; it's a bit hectic.'

'So everything is moving? Yates got the go-ahead?' Kirsty was excited by the news but thrown by the black policeman bringing tidings.

'Got to go.' Paul Leonard was the logistical guru, and all manner of tasks needed his expert attention. He turned to scramble up the path.

'Keep me informed,' Kirsty cawed as he fled.

'Let you know as much as you're allowed,' Leonard retorted, a smile and hands held high as he twisted to answer.

Craig Gayle was in custody. The children shipped, as delicately as they could be, to a relative; a policewoman who specialised in family matters playing fairy godmother. The Portuguese lover rehoused in a dingy part of East London under 'temporary police protection', a rather glamorous version of supervision.

Yates sat in a bulky loose-fitting overall on the stairs. As with all these raids, it was an early start; he'd been up since the crack. Bloody early for a man of his years. He desperately needed a fag. Paul Leonard was organising forensic crews assigned to various rooms. Shuffling outfits crackling along in their white protective garments and swishing rubber boots, unnecessarily clobbered, heavily laden with equipment. In the garden, a gang was digging by plot. Just the sort of digging you'd want in your own garden. Every bucket of soil meticulously sieved. Dogs straining on restrictive leashes snuffled and foamed. Eager young animals with saucy eyes and colossal energy. Each stage of the enquiry recorded, photographed and labelled. Collins-Maynard was right; this was an expensive business.

In no time at all the vultures were hovering. Excitable fledglings from news agencies and some grumpy, tired older men from the press. Lesser television channels had sent people who were scrambling to erect tripods and holding long booms with what resembled a dead otter at the end. Enough cameras to keep the neighbourhood buzzing.

It had been the chief superintendent's idea to team Paul Leonard with 'that curmudgeon' Yates. He wasn't sure if it was expediency or hostility. Yates held the mantle to be on the safe side. There was no way Collins-Maynard was going to look a prick over this; he knew how the commissioner dealt with failure, and he needed to clutch the reins; appear to wield power in a force that was always under scrutiny. As for the slick, young black policeman that was everything the chief superintendent expected a white policeman to be, he required a reality check. You can move too fast in the Met. It's necessary to slow down and feel the friction of some dogged police work. And this enquiry wasn't going to run smoothly; it was just the sort of mucky investigation with aggravating pitfalls that would suit Leonard. No easy ride up the ladder for this scamp.

When an excruciating morning was hitting noon, and he had drunk more coffee than was good for him, Warren Yates slipped out and stood in the furrows of the ploughed-up front garden. He wasn't going to be a martyr. He lit up. God, the sheer heaven of that cigarette. Sure he'd bite the bullet and quit later, but now this was essential; this was one of his personal commandments.

'Not much else to do but wait.' Paul Leonard was outside next to his senior officer, hands shoved in pockets, approach awkward. Apart from a formal briefing on agenda and strategy, there had been little conversation. 'When are we talking to Gayle?'

Inspector Yates wasn't comfortable when it came to building relationships. He'd had sidekicks and operational assistants, but he was a difficult cuss to get on with. Now they'd thrust a black man on him. Locked in his cracked policeman's memory, Warren recalled that you arrested black men, didn't become chummy. Warren was as flexible as a steel rod. He had compartments for everyone and all situations. 'Seems like you've got it all in hand.' The inspector dragged heavily on a rapidly disappearing dog-end and expelled a cloud of smoke away from his young sergeant. Without looking at Paul Leonard, he continued. 'We'll tackle Gayle once he's spent an incredibly worrying time in a cell. When he's tired. When he's had time to dwell on his circumstances. When he's least expecting us to charge him.' Warren Yates had his methods, had honed his interrogation skills, and knew when a man was at his lowest; at his most vulnerable.

It was dusk when the two policemen climbed into a squad car and journeyed back to Wimbledon nick. A silent trip where the two coppers scribbled reminders in their flapping notebooks.

Chapter Eight

Craig Gayle was really tired, was worried and had been processing matters when he was hauled into the interview room. He wasn't an ugly man but physically unattractive. White skin, thin red hair and moles. Many moles. Paul Leonard couldn't erase a join-up-the-dots image in his head. He would be too polite to tell anyone.

At a steel and Formica table, accommodating an ageing recording system, they sat. Warren Yates and Paul Leonard facing Gayle, owl-faced solicitor at his side. Rooms like this are bare and clinical; the voices often similar. Yates was orchestrating. Formalities were swiftly performed. Impatient to tackle the crucial issues. Paul Leonard announced, unnecessarily close to the microphone, who was in the room and the nature of the interview.

'If you could advise Mr Gayle, Sergeant Leonard,' Yates requested. He wasn't a fan of the changes that had taken place in procedure within the force, particularly the way they had screwed around with the police caution.

Gayle was informed robotically by the police sergeant. It just trips off your lips when you've repeated it so many times, and he had. Hopefully, there would be evidence to use against him.

'You are Craig James Gayle?' Yates began.

'Yes,' came the strangled reply.

'We are investigating the disappearance of Stephanie

Louise Gayle, your wife. I have several questions I need you to answer.' Warren Yates scarcely looked at the sullen man.

'When your wife went missing in October 2008, you reported her absence after a space of three days. Is that true?' Yates' tone was flat and business-like.

Craig Gayle turned immediately to his lawyer, screwing up his pale face. The grey-suited man shuffled in his chair, nodded at Gayle and faced the two policemen. 'My client has no knowledge of the questions you are intending to ask and certainly no idea how his reply might be used or possibly misinterpreted. A reasonable adviser would be far from happy to let him answer.' A tilt of the head to the nervous man.

'No comment,' Gayle mumbled, as if apologetic.

Yates and Leonard exchanged knowing expressions. There had been many, far too many interviews like this. It was imperative to ask, a case often rests on a defendant's lack of response. 'Your client is aware that failure to provide information at this time could prejudice his defence at a trial,' Inspector Yates pointed out in a weak attempt at a change of heart.

'Do you regularly take your works' vehicle home?' Yates tried again.

'No comment.'

The policeman sighed heavily. 'What was the nature of your relationship with Stephanie at the time of her disappearance?'

'No comment.'

'Were you in the process of a marital break-up or divorce? Did Stephanie have an appointment with a solicitor for the morning after she simply vanished into thin air?' Yates couldn't help adding some drama.

'No comment.'

Paul Leonard leant back in his chair and looked at the ceiling. Nothing was budging.

'At the time of your wife's absence, you were seen by the police? Is this true?'

'No comment.'

'And they spoke to you about notes that were found amongst your personal belongings? Notes that referred to the disposal of a body?'

Gayle appeared to swallow hard before answering. 'No comment,' came more from his throat than his lips.

'Do you know a man by the name of Steve Bairstow?' Inspector Warren Yates played his trump card, the joker. He waited. Paul Leonard was drawn in; now things were hotting up.

Gayle squirmed in his seat and opened his mouth to speak. Only a long silence. His crusty legal counsellor touched the faltering man's arm. Gayle looked around the room like a startled bird and sucked his top lip. 'No comment.'

And while the man was down, the policeman struck again. 'Did you ever ask this man, Steve Bairstow, if you could, for a sum, borrow or use heavy food disposal equipment that he possessed?'

Even the mild legal man murmured an audible 'shit'. It is immediately obvious when a solicitor is woken by the introduction of potential evidence that his client has conveniently failed to mention. This time Gayle was pulled hard by the arm. What had been a walk in the park had started to wade through mud. 'A moment to consult my client. Would you leave us?' The ruffled man motioned to the two officers, his face holding back a hissing scowl.

Outside, the inspector and his sergeant swapped hopeful glances. In a room full of dumb responses, Yates had scored a hit. 'Looks like he took one in the nuts with that one,' Warren Yates gleefully spluttered. 'Even kept it quiet from his brief. Now, if he denies this here, we have a big stick to beat him with, so to speak.' The policeman was showing some excitement.

Inside, Gayle cupped his head in his hands. His solicitor, a perturbed Cecil Parkinson, rustled papers and sighed and hissed. Finally, 'Well, is there something you haven't told me?' Huffing a little and intent on showing his displeasure.

Gayle stared hard at the floor, bent shoulders and rocking gently. He gulped. 'There's nothing to say.' He straightened a little. 'I know the guy. Him and his brothers run a garbage business at the market. That's it.'

'And did you approach this man concerning using his food shredder?' Parkinson studied his notes. 'Did you ask Steve Bairstow if you could use this machinery that the police are referring to?'

'No.' A flat and cracked reply.

Cecil Parkinson looked at his client over the glasses perched on his nose. 'Are there any more skeletons? Are we heading for another ambush? We have to go in there and fend off these questions, but I need to be fully armed and prepared. You are denying these matters, which could put us on the back foot if they throw them across a courtroom. It's essential we aren't wrong-footed if this goes to trial.' He'd mentioned feet too many times. It was getting late, and he was far from happy with Craig James Gayle.

No more was said. Yates and Leonard returned. Remarkably the inspector had resisted a quick fag. Paul

Leonard restarted, along with complaining mechanical growls, the old recording machine as he sat. Briefly, but more confidently, Yates explained the interview resumption to the recorder, as if it was interested.

There was definitely a degree of buoyancy to his persona as Warren Yates continued. Of course, he had another card up his sleeve. And boy was he going to have pleasure playing it. 'Mr Gayle, do you know a person by the name of Demetrio Natano?'

Who the hell was that? thought Cecil Parkinson. Immediately he turned to his client. Gayle had opened his mouth, but he didn't appear to be breathing. And certainly his eyes were locked wide open. The whole room seemed to freeze. Bodies stuck motionless. An unnerving silence.

Inspector Yates' face curled into a self-assured smirk. 'Sorry, did you not hear that? Demetrio Natano? Ring any bells?' Warren was bent on rubbing it in.

Still Craig Gayle kept his silence. Cecil Parkinson was livid, but composure, or the pretence of composure, was an essential part of a solicitor's armoury. He urged his client to blurt out a negative reply, fearing that this was, as he had dreaded, yet a further trap.

'Mr Gayle?' Warren Yates prodded.

Gayle let out all that air he had been holding on to with a gush. 'No comment.' Resignation in his voice.

Inspector Warren Yates stood, nodded in the direction of solicitor Cecil Parkinson, closed his mouth with a grin of satisfaction and announced the end of the interview. Paul Leonard turned off the recorder, removed the two tapes, scribbled details on a label, and handed one to the opposition; glad this pantomime was over.

Inspector Warren Yates had decided. A dull custody sergeant was handed Craig Gayle. 'Here's the paperwork. Murder. I'll get these files sent over to the CPS right away. We have enough.' Brutally brief; he would at least appear resolute and confident.

In the 'office', the two policemen were alone. It was late and the clerical ants that scurried around in this attic had long gone. Yates seated, Leonard perched on his desk edge. The black sergeant was not quite as pleased with himself as his boss.

'Got him in a corner,' Yates declared. 'Tomorrow we get official statements from the boy, Nicholas, queer at the market, that Portuguese batty boy and Kirsty Foster. I've got some good feelings; we're wrapping this one up at our end.' Warren Yates thrust out his chest, almost expanding with confidence. Paul Leonard had his reservations. He wouldn't air them there.

Interviews with Nicholas Gayle, Steve Bairstow, Demetrio and Kirsty were left to Paul Leonard. Inspector Yates had a senior policeman's duties to fill his day. Well, he busied himself with cleaning up his paperwork covering the interrogation of Craig Gayle and visiting the search site in Ember Lane, East Molesey. Annoyingly there was little to report. You don't find a 'smoking gun' after four years, and Warren had thought it doubtful Stephanie Gayle's body was pushing up roses in the back garden.

'The Gayle lad won't go through with this. We can use his statement, but there's no way he's turning up in court.' Sergeant Leonard slapped his folder down heavily on his slightly smaller desk next to a scribbling Inspector Yates. 'All parties quizzed, details taken and confirmed. Except for Nicholas, they'll appear. Though that Natano fellow is quaking. Nervous character, wriggling and squirming all the way through. We need to keep an eye on him.' Paul Leonard briefed his superior.

With most of the tedious work done, both men gradually realised the awkwardness of their relationship. While they had been pursuing Craig Gayle and immersed in the grind of investigation, it was nowhere near the surface. Now, sat at their individual desks scratching away at tedious paperwork, a rising difficulty nagged each policeman. A soft collision.

Inspector Warren Yates belonged to a police force that no longer resembled the institution he had joined. Sure he'd whacked a few criminals, cuffed some youths and broken a few codes of behaviour, but he wasn't a bad man. Back in those days you were a bobby, respected and feared. He'd been at the miners' strike as a young officer, driven around in screaming squad cars and nearly joined the Freemasons. There was almost a romance in the job. At his small table, he presently felt uncomfortable.

Detective Sergeant Paul Leonard was an ambitious career policeman. He had all the spunk that Yates had once possessed. Not only was the pathway planned out, but stages and landmarks had also been set. It was far from easy, and he expected a harder slog, being a black man. Racism wasn't displayed openly, yet he could often feel it dragging him back. Certain looks, on hierarchy and public faces. Diversions and obstacles that tugged at his progress. Being stuck with a narrow-minded cop from the old school was just one. Chief Superintendent Collins-Maynard knew what he was doing consigning the enterprising ethnic officer to the care of Warren Yates.

Spending his youth living in the Victorian maze of inner-suburban Tooting, Paul Leonard had been stopped and questioned more times than he'd like to remember by policemen like Yates. Probably more times than he himself had apprehended suspects. Feasibly the foundation of aspirations in this job.

In the good old days, Warren would have been heading down a dingy pub for some ales with his fellow coppers. It was out of the question to ask this assistant. He was in no hurry to head home. There was no one at home, if the cold one-bedroom flat could be called a home. When you're out all hours and called upon in the middle of the night, you soon lose the magic of a relationship. It descended into a dysfunctional awkward slide into a shared mist of no communication.

Paul was eager to leave the office and discomfort of an uneasy silence. Wife and toddler, and a book he meant to read. He cherished his home life. And in a few minutes, he would escape. What he didn't realise was that the blustering, grim detective that sat and scribbled at the slightly larger unsteady desk, was just a little frightened of him.

Warren Yates reluctantly recognised that this black police officer didn't fit the stereotype that he had stamped on his bobby's mentality. Black faces muscled around in gangs, sat around unemployed and sold drugs. Spoke and dressed loudly, and used an incomprehensible vocabulary. Stabbed each other. It was safe to suspect, search and arrest these guys. Paul Leonard had avoided the tribal gatherings on the estates and conceded to a hostile approach to education. No chip on the shoulder or attitude ingrained by downtrodden fallacies. A breath of fresh air. Yates found this disconcerting. It was difficult for the old sod to respect his young assistant at the moment. He'd wait until Leonard left the office before he trundled down the road for a drink on his own. You had to at least do that on a Friday. Home never beckoned. In fact, it was somewhere he would prefer not to go.

Chapter Nine

The Wheatsheaf could be smelled along the road, long before you arrived there. Enticing. Swirling the wafting stench of stale ale and decades of sour air. A man's pub with an odour that slapped you in the face when you pushed open the heavy oak doors. Then a cacophony of sounds; clinking glasses, shuffling customers and the scrums of professional drinkers rolling on the spot, beer glasses lodged in front or swaying from jovial hands.

Inspector Warren Yates was looking at life through the wrong end of a telescope.

Warren Yates no longer belonged in one of the scrums; he had to shuffle past the banter and the buddies to a small table away from the windows and the shadows of the street. In the past he had been a keen element of off-duty police officers, swapping tales and off-colour jokes in a raucous melee. Warren smiled a little as he carried his pint past the present groups, recalling his misspent early years in the force. A gallery of faces swung in his head. Men that had withered with illness, those that moved location or into security jobs and, glaring down at him, those that had leapfrogged Warren in the promotion stakes. A few were dead. Inspector Warren Yates, inspector was as far as he was going, because he was going soon. The only gung-ho police officer of the 90s who could barely struggle to achieve inspector status. It should have come as no surprise to Warren in his reverie that an invisible wall had been erected, a concrete wall with no way through. They often judge you on one mistake. Warren Yates had made an enormous error that curtailed any promotion.

When you organise, to the finest detail, a raid on a suspected drug baron at his spatial mansion, armed to the teeth, a fleet of heavy vehicles, you don't fuck up on location. Warren Yates did. Big time. Instead of the seedy criminals bagging up class-A drugs ready to flood the market and ruin people's lives, this seething squad arrived at a scene quite different. Sir Reginald Squires and Lady Pamela Squires, along with a splendid assembly of refined guests, were horrified to find that their cocktail party, spilling elegantly from ballroom to lawn, was being invaded by an ugly army of the Metropolitan Police. The ensuing retreat by this dark force; reversing vans, the clatter of weapons packed back in their secure cases, miserable mutterings and feeble apologies. Despite some grass damage and disturbed drive gravel little sign remained. Sir Reginald was soon on the blower to the commissioner and nailing more nails in Warren Yates' promotion coffin.

One enormous remnant, however, was the indelible stain on the service record of one Inspector Warren Yates. Not only was Warren the target of official reprimands by the hierarchy of the police force, but he was also the laughing stock for all his colleagues. Several fellow officers lived off the jokes that surrounded this infamous cockup for a long time. Warren found his own warren to hide. Gone were the chummy pub gatherings, and Inspector Yates became a shadow of his previous confident self.

Shock waves. When disasters occur in one area of your life, there are often huge ripples that splash into other areas. Warren couldn't put a date on it, yet it seemed his career error shook out what life there was left in his marriage. A wife can regularly recognise when a partner loses his attraction, a charisma sliding away, no longer the respect or admiration. Warren was a ghost, a man in the gloom of desertion and loneliness. She was seeking pastures new.

They don't just leave. Wives. They empty the coffers and grab what they can. Mrs Yates did just this. A house sold, money divided. Warren slid down the housing ladder. Small flat, big block, annoying neighbours. Further descending, almost disappearing from the far lens of the telescope.

Kids never understand, a war of blame. Warren barely saw them. Adults now, living in untroubled independent worlds. Occasionally there would be a call. Little conversation, little in common. So far down the telescope, Warren could hardly make out their faces.

Inspector Warren Yates was bitter. A bitter man with the mind-set of a 90s copper. Attitude and vocabulary of a 90s copper. Inspector Yates would leave the force with these qualities intact. Black people stereotyped, gay individuals the subject of mirth or distaste and political correctness the stuff of ridicule. It was difficult to swallow some of the present directives issued by the Yard, and Warren was often tripping over his own terminology and colourful language. An ideal candidate for the cold case loft, where he could serve out the autumn of his police career.

Much of this end of the telescope fitfully clicked through his mind. One pint would do. Warren Yates wasn't keen on drinking alone, especially when there were others truly enjoying themselves. A huddled figure leaving. At least there was work the next day to look forward to.

Work. The Gayle case was a blessing. It was the sole image that he could see from the right end of the telescope. Paul Leonard had almost broken the mould. His black assistant was growing on him. Inspector Warren Yates, hunched and shuffling, disappeared into the dismal greyness of night.

Chapter Ten

'Nothing, absolutely nothing. Fuck all!' Chief Superintendent Collins-Maynard strode across his office, head bent and clucking; with the occasional kick at a filing cabinet or two. 'All that overtime, all that fucking expense, and we add bugger all to this case.'

Warren Yates said no more. He had reported to his superior the lack of results from the search of the Gayle property. It was no surprise the old man had flown off the handle. With a commissioner who was demanding savings and cuts within the force, this chief superintendent was being hounded at every move. The Stephanie Gayle enquiry was just another casualty.

Finally, the chief superintendent slumped in his chair, still growling. He shuffled papers haphazardly. 'And, interviews, did they help? Turn up anything new? An admission, eh?' He stared at Warren Yates and jerked his head up and down. 'We're going to need more than this. I have a bloody awful feeling about this case.'

Not wishing to upset the super, Inspector Yates spoke low and flat. 'A no-comment response from the accused. But, before you explode, sir, there's some power in his silence. Not denying matters that we've put to him assists our case.' The inspector was trying to soften the blow.

'Fuck me.' Collins-Maynard sunk even lower as his feet slid under the desk. 'Witness statements?'

'All the information that we sought was confirmed.

Sergeant Leonard has made sure these are water tight.' Warren Yates was keen to get out of there.

'Leonard?' Collins-Maynard snapped and looked up. 'How's it going with the sergeant?'

Yates jiggled his head gently. 'Fine.'

The super recognised his inspector's less than enthusiastic response. 'Not really your sort, is he? Efficient and energetic, on the ball, eager and ambitious. Remember all those?' He was enjoying this. His dusty old officer who slouched over tattered files in the outbuilding next door was well past his sell-by date. He wouldn't pursue it at the moment, but there was no doubt appointing a black officer was bound to upset the wood pile.

'Without highlighting the obvious, this force has changed. You won't recall how the Met was before you arrived. Sure, there are some negative issues that stain the police at the time, but it was about real cops then.' Warren Yates was gushing and flushing, waving frantic hands. 'This politically correct namby-pampy troop that flit about in cars and don't get their hands dirty gets up my bleeding nose.'

'Quite.' Collins-Maynard had touched a nerve. For the time being there were more pressing matters. 'Getting back to this case, Inspector Yates.' He was pulling rank. 'Initially, when we reviewed this case four years ago, the CPS wasn't keen to take anything to court as there was insufficient evidence and it was not in the public interest to proceed. I'm sure you've heard this before; they fight shy of backing a loser.'

'We've got enough to crack this. Hopefully he'll snap in court. Three days before reporting her disappearance, work van at home, uncharacteristic absence, no money, passport or clothes taken, notes made about body disposal, Portuguese boyfriend and trying to commandeer a shredder that would literally make mincemeat of our Stephanie. How much more do we need?' Warren was holding on, had his finger in the dam. He wasn't about to let the bloody chief superintendent ditch this one.

Collins-Maynard took a deep breath, an audible sucking-in of a considerable amount of air. Half standing, arms on the desktop supporting his chunky leaning body. 'But, but what we fucking haven't got, Inspector, is Stephanie Gayle. No fucking body! A complete non-existence of the fucking dead.' Some of the trapped air escaped with his words, hissing. 'Our chums at the Crown Prosecution Service aren't at all happy with that. If we just had a corpse. Even an old, rotting one that some expert forensic boffin could give us half a clue from, it would be something. That sod has got rid of Stephanie for good. Without this vital piece in the jigsaw, we tread warily. CPS is as cash-strapped as we are. Have you any idea of the cost of cases like this? Stepping out on thin ice they fearfully avoid.' Collins-Maynard sat slowly, eyes closing.

Warren Yates added nothing. He collected some loose papers and headed for the door. 'Be in touch.' A swift exit.

Kirsty was at home, feeling just that little safer. On the road outside, police vehicles were occasionally passing as they decamped from the Gayle house. On site, dogs slid, mud-splattered, into vans; slobbering and excited. Handlers seemingly almost hauled in behind them. An army of investigators were disrobing; unzipping poor-fitting white overalls, and packing equipment aboard a fleet of small trucks. A team was tidying inside the house, and some work was being done to straighten the garden. Supposedly there's a policy for concluding a forensic search of a murderer's property. It was soon abandoned and locked.

Within days Craig Gayle's children arrived back at their scoured and cold home. Even the younger kids felt a little uncomfortable. Drawers in their rooms opened to find neatly folded socks and underwear, that was usually a haphazard collection of stuff. With them came an aunt who promised to stay. Social services demanded this. It would be some time before they created the chaos and added the loud voices of the old house. For the next few days there would be only whispers and ghost figures exploring; and wild imagining of what had taken place.

'They're back,' announced Justine as she scrambled into the car after school.

'Who?' Kirsty replied, attempting to be unaware.

'Murderer Gayle's kids,' Charlie chirped in.

Kirsty screwed up her eyes and bit her lip. 'Now,' she began, talking from the driver's seat to the rear of the car, 'we'll have less of that.' This wasn't going to be easy. 'Proper names and as polite as you can be. Give the children some space. Their father may have done something wrong, but we must not take it out on his kids. Understood?'

A mumbled agreement was the response from the back seat. Elliot barely paid any attention, busy reading a handout that Ms Fletcher had given all of his class. Books to read and a visit to the theatre, usual bumf.

'Abigail Gayle didn't speak all day,' Justine informed everyone. 'She's different.' There was only a smidgeon of emotion. She looked momentarily at the Gayle house as they passed. None of the children were that interested. No swarming police, far from sensational now. Their mother kept her intense concern to herself.

*

Paul Leonard was in early, scrambling up to the top floor; young enough to enjoy mornings. Rain lashed the grey streets. Yates arrived an hour later. Now it took a few coffees and a surreptitious drag before he felt human. It was his age. Neither man spoke. Paul plonked down his laptop, and Warren laid out scraps of paper. When you get to the office first, you are first to receive the news. Bad news.

'Looks like our Demetrio Natano has done a bunk,' Paul Leonard turned to mention to his inspector. 'Local copper reckons he hasn't been back to his flat for twenty-four hours.'

'Bollocks! I thought they had a tight grip there.' Yates was not pleased. 'Have they any idea where he's gone?'

'From talking to neighbours and friends, he had a few; they think he may have headed home,' Paul informed him. 'Seems like he spoke about getting away from this shit and finding a route to some small village in Portugal near Lisbon. I told you he was a wreck when I interviewed him. He's scurried off to avoid the mess that the trial will blow up.'

'I've already got the super chasing my arse. This case is fragile, and we can't afford to weaken it any more. What are you doing to trace the bastard?' Yates liked action, but he wasn't a great fan of anxiety and stress. And he was heading for both.

'Of course we've informed our friends over there. As you know, they're far from meticulous.' Paul Leonard made his way to his slightly smaller desk and lifted the lid on his laptop. Warren Yates simply gave out long hissing sighs of resignation.

'With this prick Nicholas not willing to testify, and now Demetrio has high-tailed out of it, we need to solidify Kirsty

Foster's testimony. That's all we've got if they are going to rubbish the Portuguese gay boy's evidence.' Warren Yates spoke with his head in paperwork. Yet again, he was attempting to dig this investigation out of the shit.

From not being included to suffering the constant interruptions to her rather mundane daily routine; Kirsty had the call from Paul Leonard and was clearing away the kids' litter before he came. She had warmed to the black detective. Inspector Yates huffed and forced out the occasional scowl while there was always a smile and a concern from Sergeant Leonard.

And when they sat together in the recently tidied lounge, her kindly sergeant outlined the recent developments in the Gayle case. A fruitless search of Gayle's property and the departure of a key witness. He was ready to assure her that this was nothing too severe to undermine the prospects of a successful prosecution. All was well, if not swell.

Losing such a treasured friend can have a cocktail of reactions. Kirsty had, she supposed, concentrated on the lack of progress in finding Stephanie, or discovering what had happened to her. Without realising it, and perhaps she had blocked this out, Kirsty had avoided targeting the true horror of her friend's actual disappearance and likely death. As she sat recounting the chronological details, like it was an insurance claim for a car accident, she was abruptly aware of her apparent lack of unease. Paul Leonard looked up from his papers. Kirsty's folding face and rivulet tears halted his questions.

Spluttering through a nightmare, vivid scenarios played out in her head. Was there a plan? Had Craig Gayle lain in wait for Stephanie to skip into his ambush? A hammer to the head, crushing her delicate skull? No. The blood; it would have sprayed everywhere. They'd have found that. An argument? Grabbed by the throat. His market-coarse hands squeezing the vivacious life out of her. Kirsty had Stephanie's sweet face in frame. Bulging eyes now. A silently mouthed, choking, terrified scream. Pulling with flailing hands at his vice-like grip on her windpipe. So desperate for life. Sitting after returning home? Unaware her fucked-up husband was creeping behind her. A scarf or some old rope pulled from behind. Strangling a petrified, blood-sapped face, breaking her neck. Poison or sedation? Dazed and brain swimming, swaying and lurching. Enough for Craig to push her limp or sagging head underwater in the bath. Headlight eyes submerged, mouth speaking a gabble of bubbles.

And when the so-full-of-life body was stationary dead? Had he stood back in satisfaction or delight? Water dripping from his forearms, or scarf flapping from his killer hands. A carcass. A plan for disposal. Rolled in an old carpet, a bin liner or heavy duty baggage from work. Stephanie, so impulsive, so effervescent, so exploding with vitality. A sorry limp bundle of death.

Daylight. Children rushing in from school. Concealment. Trussed up like a parcel, a mummy, awaiting dispatch. Was Stephanie stored under an accumulation of vegetable shit in his funeral van? Or, beneath a bed, in the loft between old tea chests? Ready to dump when the coast was clear. Well-rehearsed excuses and explanations for questioning eyes of young kids perched around a supper table. In the house with them. A butchered mother. All memories stolen, a mind murder blank.

No rotting corpse in the garden. Burial too difficult and inconclusive. Under water, weighed down with iron or concrete he'd brought from work? Less than a mile from the Thames. Not too difficult to dump. Like unwanted puppies at an isolated reed bank in the heaviest darkness of the miserable night. More likely the sea. A river can at times be placid, but in the ravages of the hostile ocean? Only the gormless marine life pokes around an edible corpse in the freezing depths of the main.

Merely a polite cough by Sergeant Leonard pulled Kirsty awake from the ghastly reverie. 'Are you okay?' Leonard carefully enquired. 'Can we proceed, or do you want me to come back? Another time maybe?'

'Sorry. Sometimes it hits you. All this time I've been fighting for justice for Stephanie. Haven't given much thought, until now, to what that shit did to her. Her pain.' Kirsty was slipping away again. She straightened up and appeared to shrug off the tormenting thoughts. 'I'm all right. A coffee possibly and we can carry on.'

Once again, she outlined all the relevant details of the time of Stephanie's disappearance, the visit of Nicholas and the meeting with Steve Bairstow. Kirsty kept the incursions at her back garden to herself. She had enough ghosts to deal with. Paul Leonard left with an awkward but pleasant smile.

Back in the old routine. The Foster household schedule ground on as usual. Less anxious and notably smoother. Spring was edging into summer. A trial was well in the distance. Kirsty rallied and berated the children with all the old enthusiasm and frustration. She busied herself when alone; planned and organised Tom when he was back in the country. It wasn't over, Stephanie remained in her head a great deal and peppered her thoughts, but Kirsty breathed easier, and the world was kinder.

Craig Gayle sat hunched on his metal bed. A cell, heavy with sour male breath, no bigger than the box room at home. He shared. An armed robber, Jason Costain, also on remand. Not someone he'd talk to, just the occasional grunt and troll-like exchange of scowls. Barely an hour of exercise and forever looking at the harsh painted-brick wall, sprout-green. Costain shuffled on the bunk above him, flipping through a dog-eared magazine. A festering, uneasy peace.

At the heavy steel door, the dangling of chains, the clicking of keys. 'Gayle, out. Brief's here,' a stumpy screw snapped. He led Craig Gayle down a corridor smelling of Jeyes fluid and stale food, through a series of clanking gates and to a small interview room. Airless with wafts of the fusty odour of prison kitchens.

'Mr Gayle.' A crisp-suited man rose as he entered, almost pushed into the room. 'Come, have a seat.' An open briefcase, laptop and a fan of papers filled the measly table. Meeting again, false smiles, limp handshake. Neither was a great admirer of the other. 'An application for bail. We need to go through a few things.' Cecil Parkinson of Kenwright, Smith and Ballard was keen to keep matters brief.

'Can you get me out? This place is hell,' Gayle pleadingly enquired.

'Noel Swan, the barrister we have instructed, is optimistic. They've found nothing at the house and have little more than they had four years ago. Shouldn't be a problem. Of course there'll be conditions; passport surrendered and restrictions of movement, socialising. If you keep a low profile and find someone to put up the money, Swan will get you out. Good man. Now, we know about the notes they've always had and the business with your van being at the house.' Parkinson lowered his glasses to the end of his nose. 'You've given a 'no comment' response in interview. Is there anything else you haven't told us? Swan thinks the house search and the murder charge have been initiated by new evidence or testimony. Someone's thrown something else in the pot. Our policemen friends don't waste taxpayers' money without cause. As far as we know, they're still waiting on the CPS. It will take them a while, even if they think it has legs. While this case remains wobbly, you can slip out. Keep your head down, obey the conditions, and do try to smile.'

Craig Gayle appeared to ponder. He wasn't going to divulge more. They would have to free him with what they had. 'Saying nothing more.'

Chapter Eleven

In the chaos of morning preparation that was the Foster household, the identity of any specific sound was difficult. Children milled and scampered; books, boots and lunchboxes were swung and crammed into cases and bags. Piercing voices and calming tones mingled. A doorbell missed once, rang again.

Kirsty, pestered and flustered, eventually heard the caller when they resorted to hammering on the chrome knocker. 'Sorry, getting ready for school. You know the problems.'

Paul Leonard stood, eyes lifting, face heavy, shoulders raised. 'I know it's a bit early.' He wandered into the hallway following Kirsty's beckoning gesture. Kids raced around, brushing past and hardly noticing the detective.

'What's up?' Kirsty managed to ask as she fought with her coat. 'I've got to get this lot to school.'

'We need to talk.' A policeman's serious voice.

'Look, wait here. I'll be back shortly. We'll have a hot drink and a natter then.' Kirsty had one hand on the open front door and was ushering children out and towards the purring VW with the other.

'I can sit in the car till you get back,' Leonard politely suggested.

'No, no. If I can't trust a detective sergeant.' She chuckled and slammed the door behind her.

Perhaps the worst message Paul Leonard had ever had to deliver was on the occasion of the untimely death of a young cyclist. He hated conveying bad news. It was to the boy's distraught parents. The mother had collapsed, and the father wailed uncontrollably. Quite fresh to the job, it was a long time before he was over it. What he had to tell Kirsty wasn't as bad as that, but it was going to be a bombshell all the same.

She was home after only a few minutes, intrigued to discover what news the messenger brought. 'Take a seat. Kettle will be on pronto.' Kirsty tossed her coat on the hallstand and was immediately organising the policeman.

'I'm not going to dodge this. I bear bad news, Mrs Foster. No, unfortunate news.' The brave detective was indeed sidestepping. 'Keep yourself calm.' He screwed up his mouth and looked hard into her eyes. 'With the CPS dithering, Craig Gayle was granted bail this morning.'

Kirsty sucked in all the air in the room; and held it. When she tried to speak, there was a long escaping gasp, finished with a splatter of saliva. 'What?' She shook her head and half of her body. 'How can that be? They've got enough? Surely it would be madness to let him loose?' Frantic movements. This was the worst news. She could envisage the problems ahead.

Paul Leonard tried his very best to reassure her, but some wounds are too deep for even a sweet-talking policeman to bandage. 'He's confined to the local area, not allowed near you, the school. Won't approach the children and has to constantly report to the station. I know it's far from perfect, but his brief managed to sway a knob of a judge. Sorry.' Even Paul was pissed off. 'And remember, we're here to control things and make certain you are safe and unaffected.'

Kirsty looked deep into the sergeant's dark eyes. Shutters were already being hauled down. Inside, her stomach cramped and nausea was welling up from her gut. Some device in her brain was squealing out how to cope. She kept staring at the policeman. One thing she was sure of; Tom had to come home. There was no way she could handle this devastating news without that adorable oaf.

Before the oil worker could return, Kirsty smuggled her children to and from school and kept travel to the minimum. It was the next day that feedback emerged. 'Keep getting the evils from those Gayle kids,' declared Justine once she had been coaxed into the car.

'Abigail Gayle kicked me up the bum,' Charlie innocently added. Elliot mumbled what sounded like acknowledgement and support. Kirsty took little notice and drove, her head busy with her own agenda.

Each morning followed a Groundhog Day pattern. Tom was home within a week. A wife stifled and bound by the Gayle release. Tight and edgy, far from fun. The company had found him a shitty, stifling desk job at their West End office. No more allowances for working in the bloody desert, no danger money for facing terrorist threats and no special bonuses. It would be a shock to the finances. Not much fun either. A nobody. Tom was no action-man, but he revelled in the buzz of an operational site, no matter the perilous nature of an oil well complex in the wild desert of a developing country.

Flexible hours meant Tom could either deliver or pick up from school. Other domestic stuff he would manage for the moment. Kirsty smuggled herself away and hibernated.

It was almost summer when Inspector Warren Yates was being welcomed into Kirsty's captive enclave. She forced a smile. Warren oozed apology. Coffee and the sofa. 'Next month, the fifteenth,' the supping man announced softly.

Kirsty looked up. 'For?'

'We've been through the hearings and a trial date has been set. Blackfriars Crown Court. Murder.' Warren Yates rattled out details, careful not to startle his witness. 'You'll get your summons soon. It'll be all right.'

Kirsty wasn't sure how she felt. It was certainly good to try the bastard for murder, nail him for killing poor Stephanie, but this was going to be a circus. 'You say there's been a plea hearing?'

'Yes.' Yates was dreading this.

'And?' Kirsty too had a nagging feeling cramping her colon.

'He's pleading not guilty.' Warren bowed his head, uncomfortable with his message.

'And how does he think he can get out of this?' Kirsty was on her feet, eyes alight. 'Where's the defence? What's his explanation? That arsehole killed my Stephanie. Does he believe he's getting off?'

'It's all the process. Call it justice. I know it doesn't seem like it.' Inspector Warren Yates scooped up his coat and escaped a decidedly unnerved woman.

Chapter Twelve

Airport security, guardians in crisp uniforms and the atmosphere of a government department. The odour of reams of old paper and contemporary polish. Pale wood and glass; nothing like the Dickensian sombre-ebony interior of the Old Bailey. Blackfriars Crown Court was spanking clean and bustling with the start of the week. Neat lines and the hint of a clinic. New trials awaiting the starting pistol. A huddle of confused arrivals being buzzed by paper-wielding clerks. A low noise level and some frantic meetings. Phones stuck to ears, purposeful swish of owl-legal gowns. Wigs swung in the hand on the stride, or worn at comical angles. Witnesses, nervous defendants and clusters of directing officials.

Courtroom six had the usual unassuming light-brown door with small glass window. Freshly attached, a notice read *Regina v Gayle*. An usher was fussing back and forth, ensuring all was in place. In occasional surges solicitors pushed in; wheeled bundles of documents clattered and unloaded. Attorneys arrived later, along with court officials; people who knew the routine. Falteringly the public gallery filled. Deep inside, in a serious room, an odd assembly sat or circled like birds of prey. Jurors. A motley crew was gathered and led to courtroom six, from which the parties would choose twelve thoroughly vetted candidates. Tumbling into seats. Fidgeting; some curious, some inconvenienced. Quick to fill with this high-profile case.

Quelling a tame hubbub, an usher high in the room stood.

With such a premeditated movement, recognised by most, it jolted all upright. Pacing with commitment, po-faced, came a crimson-sashed judge. His underlings nodded; he reciprocated and sat.

Up and into place, the defendant. Craig Gayle on his own in a glass-fronted dock; alone in a space that would hold a belligerent gang.

Jury in position, sworn in, barristers and lawyers dealing papers; cast of players on stage, the theatre of trial began.

A stone-featured clerk of the court read the charges. A palpable silence in the grim auditorium.

'Mr Hamilton,' Judge Richard Smithson beckoned.

'Your honour.' Crown prosecutor Sebastian Hamilton rose and smoothed his rippled gown. A sour-faced barrister not at all content with his brief, ideally severe, easing into his much-practised spiel. Hovering horn-rimmed glasses to study the script. 'Murder and prevention of the lawful and decent burial of a dead body.' Hamilton gripped the front of his gown, forcing a half-grin. Head turning, circulating the courtroom, registering the brutality of the crimes. 'It is the Crown's intention to prove to this court that the defendant, Craig James Gayle, did, on a date in October 2008, murder his wife, Stephanie Louise Gayle, and dispose of her body and thereby prevent her burial as determined by law. Mr Gayle denies this and at a previous hearing pleaded not guilty.'

Sitting further along, seemingly adopting I've-heard-it-all-before smugness, Noel Swan QC. There was enough Gayle cash to buy freedom. Even a tight-arse would pay for that. Swan charged big money. Amazing what a few high-profile successes does for your reputation and your fees. Some green junior from his chambers sat close, chasing information when necessary. A lackey to fetch notes from a scribbling solicitor.

Sebastian Hamilton lumbered through the evidence. Painting a ghastly picture. Craig Gayle was a devious killer who planned his heinous deed. Notes in Gayle's handwriting found in his briefcase proved his intention to kill Stephanie Gayle and dispose of her body. A van normally used only at work sat outside the house. The sort of vehicle you use to transport a body. Separation, divorce, financial implications; a man, knowingly prudent with his money, facing losing so much. In a marriage soured by infidelity and recrimination. 'And as we shall hear, a man capable of terrible and vile methods to hide his wicked crime.' Hamilton stalled; a Marc Antony pause. 'Such is the despicable nature of the man in the dock.' Hamilton spun around gracefully to fix his glare on Gayle.

In his chair, accompanied by a vacant-headed private security guard, Gayle was giving nothing away. Unflinching expression, arms resting on the shelf in front of him. Perhaps a quiver on his lips.

'Stephanie Gayle was the archetypal mother. As we shall learn, a mother whose devotion and love for her children surpassed all else. A mother who, the defendant will want us believe, would willingly desert them; simply disappear without money, credit card, passport. Go. Abandon those cherished young people.' Hamilton plodded through, austere and solemn. Keeping a watchful eye on each juror, knowing which one would need convincing. He was skilful at spotting those likely to be on his side. A random motley crew tugged from the general public. Experience told him who would be putty in his hands, ones he could massage in his direction.

'But, most damning will be the testament of Steve Bairstow.' Hamilton scrutinised mentally the stony defendant;

imagining cracks, even the slightest twitch. 'Mr Bairstow will tell the court the nature of the defendant's bid to organise the disappearance of his poor wife's body. A most appalling and shocking plan; sick and terrible.' Hamilton shook his head slowly, bowed and supposedly distressed.

And to get the show on the road, Sebastian Hamilton hauled Inspector Warren Yates to the witness stand to speak for the Metropolitan Police. Accepted procedure, the history of an investigation at the time of Stephanie Gayle's disappearance and contemporary decisions by assigned officers. Warren churned out the stuff. Sufficient to provide background and initial policy and action. Nothing was done. Craig Gayle was interviewed, but the force didn't have enough ammunition to go further. Shelved and filed, deep and ignored. Corpse disposal notes, possible motive and a van. What can you do with that? No body found. Nobody was interested in going further. Yates failed to mention it was force policy not to pursue such cases where the probable defendant posed no threat to the general public and there were children to be considered. 'Missing Person' was as far as they were comfortable with.

'So what changed?' Hamilton delved. 'What on earth kicked the Metropolitan Police into action? Sent a squad of officers to strip the Gayle house and excavate the garden? A sleeping dragon shaken awake, a simmering pot brought to the boil?' Sebastian Hamilton trickled out his metaphors. 'It must have been something of consequence?'

Warren Yates allowed the thought to sink in; the courtroom to absorb a pivotal manoeuvre. He knew only too well the vocal swordsmanship of this lawyer. 'Fresh evidence from Steve Bairstow, a businessman from the market. Brought to our attention was vital information that threw new light on the case, and warranted a renewed and thorough investigation.'

'Thank you,' concluded Hamilton. 'We will learn the importance of this when Mr Bairstow takes the stand. You may step down, Inspector, unless Mr Swan wishes to cross examine.' Hamilton peered across towards his adversary.

'Mr Swan?' Judge Smithson enquired.

Pulling himself upright, the tall and slender Noel Swan seemed to rise spiritually from his pew. An irksome mixture of flamboyance and arrogance. He sniffed loudly, and as if the all-seeing optic of a surveying periscope, he searched every corner of courtroom six. A slow hand smoothed his gown and brushed his trousers; a matador alone in the bullring, exceptionally confident.

'Good morning, Inspector Yates.' Cut glass syllables; a voice honed sabre-sharp. 'Cold cases being your field, I understand. You shuffle through the dusty old files that your colleagues are unable to pursue; crimes unsolved. Is that right?' Swan smiled cynically.

Warren agreed, although he felt belittled by the self-assured defence barrister. 'So are we to understand that some remarkable new material came to your attention, which persuaded you and your overlords to reopen this moribund case?'

'Yes, sir,' Warren replied respectfully.

'It must have been extraordinary to, in these difficult times, launch a full-scale search of the defendant's property? The cost exorbitant.' Swan was enjoying this. 'Funding, Inspector, funding; somebody out there is watching our every step. Ensuring we don't waste public money. It's not easy getting your superiors to back these investigations.' Noel Swan was drooling, an unpleasant smile aimed at the interrogated policeman. All too chummy to be comfortable.

'Too true,' responded Warren Yates, only too aware the direction that this barrister was heading.

'And, Inspector, would you kindly tell the court what you and your team, who rummaged and hunted through my client's property, found? What damaging and withering evidence was discovered?' Swan smirked knowingly.

'Nothing was found at the property,' Yates replied curtly.

'Nothing. Absolutely nothing. No incriminating proof was found at all. A clean sweep.' Swan swung around. 'And you pulled the defendant's property to bits, excavated his garden, dispersed his family and created havoc in the neighbourhood, for nothing. Remarkable.'

Only Noel Swan was enjoying this. Warren Yates' face was glum. Jurors were head down, scribbling notes.

Next on Hamilton's list was the crusty family solicitor who confirmed, without emotion, the deteriorating state of the Gayle marriage and the appointment set to discuss the process of separation and divorce. Noel Swan had no questions.

Kirsty Foster took centre stage. An engaging witness who spoke volumes about the loving mum and fantastic friend who abruptly disappeared without trace or explanation. Quite out of character and in no way a devoted friend and mother would behave. Entirely credible testimony. Sebastian Hamilton stood like a proud rooster as Kirsty painted a vivid picture of her soul mate and the disintegrating marriage she was trapped in. There was no way Craig Gayle wasn't an arsehole and a killer. 'And if the police had asked me at the time, things may have been different.' Kirsty was tearful at the end. It was indeed a huge relief, at last, to unload the emotional burden she had carried for so long. A four-year blanket shadow clogging the very ordinariness of life.

Noel Swan QC was going nowhere near her. A tearful woman has swayed many a juror. You don't need that. Kirsty blubbing would set his case way back. With a wave of his hand and a simple, 'No questions, your honour.' The quicker the woman left the scene the better.

Now Sebastian Hamilton was ready; a shuffle of his feet and stretched body language showed it. The coup de grâce. A hush followed Kirsty as she tumbled from the witness box. Only some low clearing of throats and the movement of tired limbs.

'The next witness for the prosecution is Mr Stephen Bairstow.'

An usher strode out to hail and escort Steve Bairstow to the stand. A Bible was thrust into his hand, and he read gruffly from a card. Formalities done with, Steve stood, tilted head and spaniel eyes. In the solid oak box, his wiry frame even thinner, sparse hair obviously smarmed over the glossy skin of his bony head. Ill-fitting new suit and clumsy bulging tie knot. A stranger to smart appearances.

'You are Stephen Bairstow and you work at New Covent Garden market. Is this true?' Hamilton opened.

'Yeah,' Steve gurgled, not yet ready to converse.

'Please tell the court, Mr Bairstow, how you know the defendant.' Hamilton proceeded slowly. Nothing to be missed.

''e works there,' Steve bluntly responded.

'Alongside you, doing the same job?' continued Hamilton.

'No, 'e runs a fruit and veg business; sells to outlets and stores. I, well, me and me bruvvers, we 'ave a clearance firm. Dump rubbish, remove all the market trash. There's lots of that.' Steve was finding words easier.

'And, Mr Bairstow, tell the court how this is done, your methods and procedures,' Hamilton added.

'Procedures? It ain't very tricky. We picks up the waste goods and packaging that's lying around on a busy market day. Most of it's shoved through one of our shredders, and the mush and debris is loaded into containers and we dump it. Official like, we aren't yer cowboys leaving it anywhere. Landfill and incineration. It's all sorted before a decided destination, so to speak.' Steve was in an area he knew well, sounding almost professional.

'This machinery you use, it sounds really robust and efficient.' Hamilton appeared very impressed. Steve only nodded with the hint of a smile.

Ready to wave his stick and bubbling with something like glee, Hamilton asked his killer question. 'Cast your mind back, Mr Bairstow. In the October of 2008, did the defendant, Craig Gayle, approach you concerning this machinery?'

'Yeah.'

'Please tell the court the nature of your conversation.' Sebastian Hamilton rubbed his hands.

'We 'ave a powerful shredder what is used for large and difficult jobs, you see. We calls it the Mangler. Gayle asks me if 'e can borrow it. Rent it to get rid of some rotten foodstuff, foreign fruit that was stinking the place out. I told 'im 'e could. I'd 'ave to show 'im 'ow to use it. Couldn't control that beast on 'is own. Wanted it for a weekend. Keen to know where the stuff would be dumped.'

'And did the defendant borrow this machine?' Hamilton asked.

'No. Wanted to work it 'imself. This machine is a beast; I weren't 'aving that.'

'When you heard of Mr Gayle's wife going missing and the mystery surrounding this disappearance, didn't you put two and two together? Weren't you at all curious?' Hamilton jabbed. 'I'm certain the jury will have some concern, and rightly so.'

Noel Swan fidgeted in his seat but said nothing.

Steve continued. 'Sure, I thought about it. Markets are tribal; we don't start shooting our mouths off. Tight ship at New Covent Garden. Wouldn't of said nothing.'

'Looking back. Do you consider it possible the defendant was considering using your, what is it, Mangler, to dispose of his wife's body?'

Noel Swan was up now. A twitching sparrow head and whistle to his voice. 'Objection, my lord.'

'Yes, yes.' Judge Smithson was quick to react, well aware of the scenario. 'Mr Hamilton, I will not permit this. Mr Swan is correct in his objection. You are asking your witness to express an opinion, a supposition. This is clearly unacceptable, and the jury is directed to ignore this question.'

'Apologies.' Sebastian Hamilton had succeeded. All he needed was for the jury to follow, to put the idea into their heads. No judgement could erase this concern. He had, as had Swan, played this out several times in other cases. As with so much of the courtroom shenanigans it was part of the duel, an essential in the gladiatorial hostilities of a trial. 'Let me rephrase my question. Is this machinery that you use at the market capable of mincing up a human body?' Hamilton eyed the bench to catch the reaction of the judge. 'Reducing it to a mere sludge and fragments?' Indeed he wanted the jurors to imagine the horror.

'Thank you, Mr Hamilton,' Smithson interjected. He wasn't having any more pictures like that painted in his courtroom.

Nervously, Steve Bairstow waited for the exchanges to settle before he tried to speak. 'Crush anything; a real brute. Sure it would do all that damage. That's why we 'ave to be so careful using the bleeder,' he explained, verging on chirpy.

With a quick nod to the jury, Hamilton snapped, 'No further questions.' And promptly sat. It was important to leave that gruesome image fixed in those very normal people's heads.

'We will adjourn unless you are going to be quick in your cross-examination, Mr Swan,' announced the judge.

Swan leaned across to his opponent, Sebastian Hamilton. 'We are both of the opinion that an adjournment would be welcomed. I do not, at this point, wish to question the witness. However, I request the court's permission to re-examine his evidence at a later stage.' Hamilton nodded to Judge Smithson.

'In that event, this completes the case for the prosecution, if that assists your honour,' Sebastian Hamilton announced.

'Perfect. Good timing.' Smithson rose. All bodies in the room followed. A quick gesture and he was gone. Striding through his convenient door close to the bench. A beak's prerogative.

The same milling about and groups of muttering lawyers mustered the next day. Kirsty Foster, now she had said her piece, was in the line of onlookers that filed joltingly into the public gallery. Choosing a seat where she could see Craig Gayle clearly, but where he hopefully wouldn't notice her. Jabbering chaos and flitting figures in the main body of the room until the special door opened and an usher declared the appearance of Judge Richard Smithson. There were matters to deal with before the session began in earnest. A convenient late start for many.

'Mr Swan,' Smithson introduced.

As an ego-resplendent old actor climbed from his seat and entered the stage, feeling the eyes settle on him. Somewhat Shakespearian and certainly overtly thespian. Noel Swan QC was in his element.

'Defence. A troublesome chore at the best of times.' Swan had his own way of presenting a drama. 'You have heard from my colleague some extremely harrowing stuff. Ordinarily it would be difficult for anyone to argue a case against such compelling testimony. Fortunately for me, and for the defendant, much of what you have heard warrants a not guilty verdict.

'Beyond all reasonable doubt. That's what you have to decide.' Swan surveyed the peculiar mix of the public that made up the jury. 'Mr Hamilton has had to persuade you that my client, beyond a reasonable doubt, killed his wife, Stephanie Gayle, and disposed of her body. I know Craig Gayle did not do these things. This I will demonstrate to you. Listen carefully to the evidence; a man's freedom depends on it.' Almost a hangman's severity to his face.

'This is a charge of murder. Murder? Who has been murdered? Are we certain that Stephanie Gayle was murdered, as they say, in October 2008? Where is the corpse? I am only too aware how distressing this woman's disappearance is to her family; five adoring children and a grieving husband. Yes, the defendant Craig Gayle, hurts just like so many others. He is no killer.

'Stephanie went missing, that's true. Out of the blue, she simply vanished. But we are ignorant bystanders who must rely on the people there at the time. Did Stephanie feel it was all too much and walk out the door? Start a new life somewhere away from the stresses of her marriage? A new life with someone else? Is she out there now? Have you or I passed her in the street, blissfully unaware of who the bustling lady is? Fresh people, fresh place, fresh country? Who can tell?' Swan sighed and paused. A jury needs time for ideas to sink in; for notions to germinate. 'So we try this unfortunate man for murder. A murder that the prosecution asks you to accept has taken place, without a dead body, and, importantly, without any real supporting evidence.'

Louder and almost heralding a messiah's arrival, Swan waved an arm. 'I call Craig Gayle to the witness stand.'

Amidst a gentle murmuring, Craig Gayle made his way from the dock to the pulpit-like witness booth central to the courtroom. Not a small man, but slightly bent as if humbled; head forward, wispy ginger hair flapping slightly as he climbed into the box.

Noel Swan began. And he knew how to massage the best from his clients. Asked about the incriminating notes about body disposal found in Craig Gayle's possession, he was well-practised and thoroughly rehearsed for the performance. It had been a time of marital disharmony, stress and depression. A period of dark thoughts, nothing else. There was no way he was enacting these ideas or truly considering concealing or dumping a body.

'The jury will fully understand that there is a huge gap between fancies and real intention,' added Swan. 'Who hasn't jotted down the most ludicrous of concepts only for them to remain as pipe dreams on forgotten scraps of paper?'

Craig Gayle was a tight arse, of that there was no doubt. Swan's questioning, far from exposing that, painted a picture of a careful businessman, honest worker, wise investor and providing efficient husbandry for his family. Dressed up holy and down-playing accusations by Sebastian Hamilton that Gayle held on to his marriage to avoid dishing out his funds. Then even some of the great masters' works are found to be skilful fakes. A series of well-designed questions that Gayle could answer persuasively had him smelling of roses. Sound and shrewd with the household purse; no suggestion of the true skinflint.

Swan changed tack. Playing a trump card. With a shrug of his shoulders to rearrange his slipping gown, he breathed in heavily. It was important he played this right. 'Mr Gayle, would you kindly tell the court the state of your marriage to Stephanie at the time of her disappearance.'

Craig Gayle spoke heavily, head down, muffling some of his testimony. 'We weren't getting on. She had talked about a split. I had issues. Think she was seeing a couple of blokes; a plumber who did some work for me, Phil, and a gardener prick by the name of Rory. Don't know how serious this was.'

'Were these Phil Lowe and Rory Pritchard?' supported Swan.

'Yeah.'

'Your marriage was troubled and possibly heading for breakup, is that true?' Swan went further.

'Yeah.' Gayle was jabbing out, short and sharp, his reply.

'Do you know a person by the name of Demetrio Natano, Mr Gayle?' Swan asked.

'Yeah.' Gayle gulped.

Judge Richard Smithson looked concerned. In his court, he was a stickler for procedure and relevance. Sebastian Hamilton felt the perspiration form beads and inch down his forehead.

'How do you know Mr Natano?' Swan proceeded.

Gayle struggled to speak. 'Works, or did work, at the

market.'

'To you? What did Mr Natano mean to you?' Swan was almost there. Seconds from the killer blow.

Craig Gayle appeared to breathe only through his nose, an audible snuffing sound. He had been far from articulate, but now he was barely able to communicate. 'Good friends, like.'

'Isn't it true that you and Mr Natano were, in fact, in a sexual, or should I say a homosexual, relationship?' Swan almost bellowed.

As if disturbing a hive of working bees, the courtroom broke into a buzzing of muttering voices. Eyes widened and heads twitched.

Richard Smithson, from his high chair, rapped his gavel. 'Mr Swan, where is this line of questioning going? I am finding it difficult to recognise its significance.'

'Bear with me, your honour. The defence case heavily relies on the matters we are soon to hear about. Be assured that my line of enquiry is well within the constraints of this case.' Swan displayed a horrible smile, appearing to virtually drool.

'I ask you again, Mr Gayle. Were you and Demetrio Natano in a homosexual relationship?' Swan swung back to his client.

'Yeah.' Gayle arched even lower. He gulped. As if dragging from a great depth this torturous secret.

'Can you confirm to the court, difficult as it may be, that in spite of a long marriage and the rearing of children, you and Mr Natano were lovers? That you are, in fact, bisexual?' Very matter-of-fact but decidedly rewarding. Noel Swan was in his element, setting a trap.

Gayle looked around him. At the condemning eyes and the glower, startled. His face was seemingly greyer, and his posture was that of a man sinking through his crumpling body, trying to disappear into that very public witness box.

A simple, 'Yes.' Like stabbing himself.

'No further questions,' Swan snapped as he sat.

'Mr Hamilton?' asked Judge Smithson, offering the prosecution a timely examination.

Sebastian Hamilton shook his head. 'No, your honour.' There were possibly some matters that the prosecution could have raised, but Hamilton knew he had to get the grubby man out of the witness spotlight as quickly as he could. He was well aware of the defence's strategy. A trap was looming.

Verging on an interlude, after Craig Gayle's explosive admission, Swan cross-examined the two men who had allegedly had affairs with Stephanie. If true, she obviously hadn't been that fussy. Both were rough diamonds. Men who worked with their hands and less with their brains. Malleable to the clever tongue of the barrister. Summoned attendees; not at all happy they had been dragged there.

Rory Pritchard was a gardener, even though his flyers claimed he was *a master of horticultural design*. It's what you did, inflate your competence. Noel Swan dragged out the messy details of a grubby affair that wasn't going anywhere.

'I'd stopped seeing her months before she vanished,' he declared. It was enough to besmirch the missing woman's character. Enough to raise the jury's feelings towards the pitiful accused man. Kirsty, way back in the public gallery, found it hard to listen to.

'Now let me see. You have worked in the garden of remembrance at that vast cemetery near Woking?' Swan fiddled with his papers. 'A sprawling place, Brookwood. Yes, that's the one. You have a contract to keep the weeds down, I believe?'

'I have,' Rory replied in a 'so what' tone.

'Just out of interest, and not at all being controversial, wouldn't it be easy for you, while working, to slip an extra body into an open grave there without anyone noticing, if you are clever?' Swan dared to dangle a likely, yet unlikely possibility.

Judge Richard Smithson looked daggers at the lawyer. 'And where is this leading us, counsel?'

'Apologies, your honour, a mere enquiry.' Swan gave a naughty boy grin.

'Move on,' Judge Smithson urged. 'Keep it relevant to the case. I trust you were not pointing a finger?'

'Most certainly not, your honour. Simply exploring endless possibilities.' Swan examined papers before dismissing Pritchard. Sebastian Hamilton wasn't going to pursue this witness. Judge Smithson was finding the defence barrister a pain in the arse. Not that he would use such an expression.

Phil Lowe was perhaps a little too pretty to be a plumber. But then the court couldn't see the 'booze-inspired' tattoos that laced his arms and illustrated his skinny legs. They had fascinated Stephanie. She had often spent time tracing the swirls and loops with her fingers during some sordid trysts. The plumber was a diversion. She had needed that.

'Mr Lowe,' began Noel Swan, 'you were involved with Stephanie Gayle at the time of her disappearance. Did this sudden apparent vaporisation concern you?'

'It weren't serious. A bit of fun. I knew Steph were married, like.' Lowe's reluctance was showing through. 'Thought she'd got tired. Perhaps found someone else. Anyway, I weren't short of women to see.' Phil Lowe wasn't going to let people know he had been dumped.

'Charming,' snorted Swan. 'And these years later, anything troubling you?'

'Just thought, like everyone, that her old man had done her in.' Phil Lowe picked his nails, down-to-earth, unbothered.

'Members of the jury,' interrupted Judge Smithson, 'kindly ignore that last remark. Keep opinions to yourself, Mr Lowe.'

'Precisely, your honour,' trumpeted Noel Swan, 'such speculation is unwarranted and untrue. In fact, Mr Lowe, with all these ladies after your body, perhaps Mrs Gayle was a burden, on the older side? Were you tired of Stephanie Gayle and wanted to move on? Did Stephanie Gayle's disappearance suit you, set you free?'

Awoken and flustered, Phil Lowe gasped. 'What? You reckon I bumped her off? Is that what you're saying?'

'I am saying nothing. I simply asked you if this affair was on its last legs. I suggest that you were unconcerned about the fate of the poor woman. Would that be the case?' Swan was percolating the minds of jurors in his inimitable way.

'It wasn't a big deal at the time. Didn't know she'd been done in, did I? Didn't bloody kill her.' Phil Lowe was feeling picked on.

Swan sat. Enough done.

It had been an enlightening day. Judge Smithson was weary and proceedings were brought to an end.

A fresh morning, and one the defence team had been waiting for. Noel Swan was buoyant. Quick to rise, once the dust and the dusty had settled in Court Six. Black and white; a magpie figure, swirling the wings of his robes. Papers were rustled and coughs muffled into paper-cupped tissues as a full courtroom squirmed themselves comfortable.

All the players assembled. Teams in place. Judge Smithson

signalled the kick-off.

'At this point, your honour, I would like to recall the prosecution witness, Mr Stephen Bairstow. You will recollect I explained to your honour that I withheld the opportunity to question this man at the time and that matters would be raised later.' Swan held back excited dribble threatening to slide from his mouth.

'Yes, Mr Swan. Carry on.' Judge Smithson was often irritated by the tactics of some of his legal chums. Sebastian Hamilton sat uneasily. Warren Yates and Paul Leonard almost hissed as they sucked in a little more air than usual. They were savvy enough to recognise Swan's intention.

Steve Bairstow assumed a spidery appearance in the witness box. Seeming even thinner and stooping further. His gaunt face skin heavier and deeper lined, and now a shade of grey.

'Mr Bairstow, sorry to haul you back here,' Swan declared, not at all honest in his apology. 'I just need to clarify some points. The defendant, Craig Gayle, has told the court that he knew a Demetrio Natano. Let's say, knew him intimately.' Swan held his lips firm to foil a grin developing. 'Did you know Mr Natano?'

Jerking nervously, Steve Bairstow wriggled with his mouth and the bungling words. 'Yeah, I knew 'im.'

'Kindly tell the court how you knew Mr Natano.'

'Worked at the market. 'elped run a stall.' Muffled words from a reluctant witness.

'I see,' Swan acknowledged, 'and what truly was your relationship with Mr Natano?'

'Relationship?' Bairstow strained.

'Yes; isn't it correct you were friends with Demetrio

Natano?'

'Yeah.' Some safety in that admission.

'Demetrio Natano, a young, athletic youth from Portugal. Fresh-faced, blue-eyed, high-spirited and fun to be with, wouldn't you say?' Swan smirked.

Steve Bairstow held on tightly to a picture in his porridge-filled head. Bronzed, toned and excited, black-sleeked hair and inviting grin. How he had adored that boy.

'Would I be correct in saying that you are a gay man, Mr Bairstow?' Swan continued.

'Yeah.' Steve closed both eyes as if to hide his answer. As if it were visible.

'Did you begin a sexual relationship with Demetrio Natano?' Swan dilly-dallied no further. 'Isn't it a fact that you and Mr Natano were a couple, and that you were in a homosexual association with this man for several months?'

A weighty silence, and people stuck stationary as if in a game of statues. All the spicy thoughts unspoken, and not even an innocent movement to scratch a nose. The jurors nodded their heads slightly, rocking forward as though getting closer to the spicy bits.

'Yeah, we was.' Steve Bairstow could have continued and told of his love for his Portuguese Adonis. Of the beauty of their time together. It was a rare bloom in a desperate life. His deep thoughts were quickly punctured.

'Mr Bairstow, please tell the court why this relationship came to an end.' Swan rotated on the spot, his face annoyingly fixed with a glow of supreme satisfaction.

'It was Gayle. Craig Gayle stole 'im. Ruined everything, 'e did.'

It was out. Without having to squeeze his victim, the

destructive evidence was singing around the gawping room. 'So you are telling the court that the defendant, Craig Gayle, and Mr Natano became an item? That Craig Gayle destroyed your dream, stole Mr Natano, devastated your life. Didn't he?' Swan's brutal words.

'Yeah, 'e did.'

'Thank you, Mr Bairstow.' Swan rested, turned some pages and adjusted his scratchy wig. He loved it when a plan came together.

'You will remember, and I can remind you if you wish, that you told the court that Mr Gayle had asked to... let's see what you said.' Swan swished through his pile of documents until he found what he wanted. Arranged his best plastic cockney accent, '"*the mangler. Gayle asks me if 'e can borrow it*". That's what you told us. Do you remember?'

'Yeah.' If he could have slipped further down into that monolith of a witness box, he would have; how he wished to disappear along with his misery.

'Jurors.' Now Swan turned to his real audience. 'Members of the jury take note. Woe, a lover spurned is a volatile beast. A lover scorned will act unpredictably and understandably reckless.' Swan whipped about and returned to the ghost in the witness box. Like some rank prey that thought it had been shaken and bloodied, wrung of all sense. Slumped listless.

'Is it not true, Mr Stephen Bairstow, that in rage and jealousy, in distress and retribution, you invented this story for the court? You blatantly fabricated this conversation with the defendant, didn't you? Craig Gayle never approached you concerning the use of your shredding machinery. This was merely a reaction to the pain and wretchedness he caused you, wasn't it?' Swan stretched his neck and wheeled round the room like a searching periscope. Mouth shut firm and eyes glaring.

The sodden mass that was Steve Bairstow scrumpled and shaken in the light oaken box, who ironically had been, by words, mangled beyond recognition, became the centre of all attention. 'Mr Bairstow, defence council requires a reply.' Judge Smithson was also eager to hear.

'Asked me... told you. Gayle asked to borrow it.' Steve struggled to flop out the words.

'No further questions.' Swan almost spoke at the same time. Plonked himself down and bent over his papers.

'After a break, which we all need, and assuming neither counsel requires to call further witnesses, we will hear closing speeches.' Judge Richard Smithson rose, and the groaning courtroom rose with him.

Kirsty waited until the bulk of the crowd had left. She loitered in the corridor, pausing for the arrival of Warren Yates and Paul Leonard. Teammates with negative body language. In the panto finale, Swan had proved a better performer. They slunk off to the canteen for tea and solace.

On resumption, a stage now left to the principal actors. Sebastian Hamilton and Noel Swan QC had presented their cases, and each was determined to bind it all up with their most eloquent delivery. Last chance saloon.

Hamilton spoke first. Concentrate on the strong points and hammer home evidence that hurts the defendant. That's the technique. So, Sebastian Hamilton reintroduced the notes that Craig Gayle had written, the completely out-of-character disappearance of Stephanie and her motherly concern for her wonderful children, Gayle's stinginess and the prospect of financial ruin. Of his vile and despicable attempt to hire equipment capable of chewing up that poor woman. 'No body. No smoking gun. We do not know where the remains of this dear lady now lie. Mr Gayle does not tell us, but be assured this man holds that wicked secret. Only he was responsible for her death and vanishing without a trace. Of this there is no question. You twelve citizens must decide. The prosecution has shown you that there is no reasonable doubt about the defendant's responsibility. Only one verdict will provide justice for Stephanie Gayle.' Hamilton fixed a hangman's sneer on his flabby face. 'Guilty.' Hamilton dropped to his perch.

'Fine words indeed,' Swan agreed. He approved of much that had been argued and how valid was a great deal of what Hamilton had said. 'And if that was all, the complete bundle, then surely my client is guilty. Serious facts point to some mischiefs and appalling thoughts by the defendant. His wife's disappearance at a time when their marriage was rocky and splitting apart did not bode well. 'Except.' Arrogance on his smug face. 'Except for the loathsome power of revenge. Yes, dear jurors, this is where this case is hinged. A pivotal element. Mr Stephen Bairstow has, as do injured people, succumbed to the dangling carrot of retaliation. This man invented a conversation so salient to the prosecution case, solely because Craig Gayle stole his great love. Demetrio Natano swapped Mr Bairstow's bed for that of the defendant. And Steve Bairstow could not forgive him, could not recover from this dreadful act of betrayal. Revenge was his only weapon. And he has used it now. Brutally, in my opinion, he fabricated this fearful lie.' Swan shook his head at the severity of the act. 'Only a not guilty verdict will suffice. Prosecution counsel has not proved, beyond reasonable doubt, that Craig Gayle killed his wife, Stephanie. Missing, of course, is Stephanie Gayle's body. There is no forensic evidence of her death, and she could well be living a new life, unaware of her husband's dilemma or not caring a damn. It would be inconceivable if you, for a moment, thought he slaughtered this woman. True justice relies on your trustworthy decision. Thank you.'

Judge Richard Smithson had watched too many gladiatorial lawyers squirm away below him. Boy, he was in a position to have awarded Oscars for performance from his experience. Swan had played the part exceptionally well. He was aware how the jury would poll. A judge's summing up needs to discriminate relevant from red herring. Pull the evidence and testimony together that has been thrown around his court and present a ready-cooked version that is palatable for a jury's consumption. And so Judge Smithson ran through it all again, emphasising those areas where the opportunity occurs for these fine folk to make decisions. He smiled at times; on other occasions his owl brows and eyes piercing through dark-rimmed spectacles took a sombre turn. 'Has the prosecution been able to demonstrate, beyond reasonable doubt, that the defendant, Craig Gayle, has indeed killed his wife Stephanie and disposed of her body? That Stephanie Gayle is actually dead? That is the essence of your decision,' Smithson briefed. 'Or had Mr Swan provided sufficient doubt to the defendant's guilt? You may consider he was able to show that the evidence of Stephen Bairstow is not to be relied upon. If that is the case, there is, I have to say, a sound reason to acquit.

'We have no body, no dead Stephanie Gayle to examine for clues to the cause of her death or evidence to secure the culprit involved. Members of the jury, take your time; take all the time that you need. And when you feel that you are ready, return to this courtroom and present your decision. May truth guide you and wisdom persuade you. A jury has a most serious and onerous duty. My thoughts are with you.'

Much like a wedding-seating usher, the court attendant led the twelve just people from their two-tier pew and into the vacuum of an austere deliberation room. Verdict awaited.

With legal presence and arthritic caution, Smithson rose. The courtroom emptied. A long and lingering pause.

A jury is a complex mix of assorted characters. Its members shuffled out and were escorted to a far room where, securely locked away, they ploughed through the many aspects of the case. There were several who 'didn't like the man' and others who felt 'he wouldn't do that'. For several hours and many cups of tea, the foreman, a bespectacled man of indefinite age, led them through the evidence and its relevance. With little persuasion they finally agreed. You are never sure that this decision is derived from a concern for justice or a desire to return to family and normality as soon as possible. An usher was marshalled to inform the court that a verdict had been reached.

Chapter Thirteen

'Not guilty.'

Handcuffed silence. Barely a breath. Craig Gayle's face hardened into a self-satisfied smirk.

'Not guilty.' The jury foreman mumbled out their decision on the second charge.

Judge Richard Smithson closed shop. Thanked the contestants, released the defendant and dismissed the jury. Duty done, they didn't spare the horses and gladly headed home. He failed to thank the British public for forking out the money to pay for this unsuccessful prosecution. A judge had to appear above such mundane yet practical matters.

Noel Swan packed away papers and closed books. Smug wasn't the word for it. He edged his way along the front bench to the still-seated Sebastian Hamilton. A contest over, they exchanged the pleasantries of welterweight boxers at the bell. But Hamilton hated losing to that ego-primed lawyer; he'd drown out defeat with some hefty shots of Glenmorangie in his musty study later.

Detective Inspector Warren Yates did not speak. Detective Sergeant Paul Leonard did not speak. They waited in the cooler corridor for Kirsty. Neither spoke. They silently kicked at ghosts. A fury of silence only broken by the exhaling of tormented air through gritted teeth.

'So he's off. Got away with it. We won't find Stephanie now.' Kirsty gabbled to the speechless policemen. 'How could they let that killer go?'

Yates and Leonard did their best to comfort a defeated soldier. How she had battled on behalf of her friend. She would lope back home in the same dumbstruck disbelief as her crestfallen police officers.

Chief Superintendent Collins-Maynard stormed around his fine office, scaring young officers who were anywhere near. Heads were to roll; a scapegoat outed, an albatross hung round his neck. And in they walked. Feeling like casualties, treated like villains. 'Yates and Leonard, sit down.' Collins-Maynard barked. Two more circuits of the fine office before he spoke again. You couldn't be sure if it was to build up the venom or organise his thoughts.

'There was a time when it was simplicity itself. We had a bad guy and we sent him down. No shit with the courts; everything could be fixed. You remember those days, don't you, Warren?' The chief super was easing into this bollocking, making his colleagues feel foolishly comfortable.

Warren Yates muttered an agreement; Paul Leonard, for no reason except nerves, nodded.

'All in all,' Collins-Maynard grabbed at some papers, 'we have, the country has, spent six hundred thousand pounds on achieving Jack Shit. Money we cannot afford to waste has been flushed through the system like a fucking turd!' He rose again and wandered around his fine office, waving the accounts. 'We don't have the luxury of seeing our man sent down, assured of a long sentence; know he's out of circulation until he's a fucking old man. No, we have to make sure we have, above board, all the evidence and testimony to ensure the villain has this hung over him, is found guilty by his fucking peers!'

The chief superintendent landed back into his chair. 'You

two doughnuts fucked up. Big time. The commissioner is going to have my guts for garters for this. Both of you useless dicks can cosy up side by side forever in that morgue of an office next door. It's paperwork upon paperwork for you two. No cold case reviews do you follow; become bloodhounds. Pass anything on to my officers. We'll decide where we go and when we stop. This is the last time I listen to your crap.' Collins-Maynard ushered the two policemen out with a sweep of his hand, still condemning them with a furious glower filling his enraged face.

Paul Leonard and Warren Yates, well-practised at the no-talking, crept up to a corner of the busy little office next door and did their best to hide at their Spartan desks. Warren sat for only a few minutes before sliding off for that essential deep draw from a fag.

'When does this shit stop hitting the fan?' queried Paul Leonard when his boss returned. 'I didn't join the force to sit around pushing my pen and searching through a graveyard of files going nowhere.'

'Time. It'll be a matter of time. You'll be back out there soon. They'll probably put me out to graze.' Warren was resigned, yet again, to a hermit's life. A discarded possession hauled to and abandoned in the annexe attic, much like the rest of his existence.

Craig Gayle was elated. A fresh exuberance and sporting the body language of victory. Unfairly chased and prosecuted by the police and hidden voices, by people he knew, people that he knew where they lived, people who thought he'd murdered his wife. And people who had turned up in court to try and jail him, try to remove him from his house, from the neighbourhood, from the kids. Now, he would make the most of his presence and his innocence.

Tom took the children to school. Kirsty couldn't face Gayle's bubbling ego and strident flaunting of his much-hailed virtue. Tom disliked Craig Gayle, but he merely ignored the arrogance and self-righteousness the man now displayed for the benefit of bundles of mothers delivering and collecting pupils.

For Kirsty, leaden days, fitful nights. Withdrawn and barely coping. She had decided, in her tidy mind, that Craig Gayle was going down, neatly jailed. A long prison sentence that removed him from her life; a closure. At last, Stephanie's killer would be behind bars, and all would be well with the world.

Not so.

Hardly bothering to dress, she would spend far too long bound tightly in a thick dressing gown, foetal, in a deep, but not deep enough, armchair. Battling her demons. Revisiting the brutality of life.

And in those woken, grey, silent hours, when Tom was blustering and wrestling his own slumber dragons, she continued to pursue her torments. By morning Kirsty had fallen into a quicksand of sleep. Deep and full of strangling terrors. That morning the moaning of the shed door roused her consciousness. When it really mattered, she had asked her reluctant husband to oil the bleeding thing; he never did.

Why was Tom in the shed? What was the time? He's never in the garden in the morning? A bombardment of testing thoughts. Kirsty struggled to the window. Tom saw her. It was meant to be a silent chore, kept from her fragile state, away from her fretful eyes. But she saw it. The night time visitor had ghosted in once again. Central, in the neat lawn, black and menacing in the shade; a grave. Shallow, dug agonisingly accurately, a rectangular pit, piled soil at the side to fit a body. Tom squirmed at the sight of Kirsty seeing it. Pain curling her face. He hurried with the spade grabbed from the shed. Filled the hole as quickly as he could. A patchwork of hastily placed turf. He trod it down. A frantic repair. He realised it was a pathetic attempt to cover the evidence. Once he had finished, he scrambled indoors; arms encasing his quivering wife.

'Fucking Craig Gayle.' Kirsty blubbed. 'He's started again.'

'I'll deal with him!' Tom seethed. 'He'll pay for this.'

'No. I couldn't be without you. If you attack him, they'll sling you in prison. That'll be just what he wants.' Kirsty pulled at her husband's threatening arm that was raised in anger, pumping the space between their house and Gayle's.

Two phone calls. Tom made certain the police were involved this time. He wanted to beat the shit out of Gayle; this was the best he could do. Kirsty's whimpering call was to the two damned police lepers. Warren Yates and Paul Leonard, still smarting from the severe berating by Chief Superintendent Collins-Maynard, listened to her. It hurt. They were helpless. Collins-Maynard was bristling and wouldn't revisit or touch this case with a bargepole.

'Kirsty, keep strong.' Warren Yates did his best to comfort the sniffling woman. 'Gayle's playing with fire if he tries this again. Local force should make a visit. Warn him; he wouldn't dare risk being dragged back to court. And, most of all, don't let that bastard intimidate you.' Warren knew his words were flaccid and apologetic. His hands were tied.

Tom spent a long time repairing the lawn. His initial hasty work had been clumsy and rushed. Now he ensured this was a top cosmetic job. A present for Kirsty. As he toiled he deliberated. Kirsty was not going to continue a vigil outside Gayle's house; he'd be firm about that. Neither would he consider working abroad again. No matter how much of a rut he felt he was edging his way into. Anyway, sub-Saharan West Africa was sliding dangerously into near-chaos. He'd be more of a father to Charlie, Justine and Elliot. More of a husband. Reluctantly someone the family could rely on. Took him long enough to grow up.

Chapter Fourteen

Time, ah time. We all know what they say about the healing nature of time. And in the Foster household, time was doing its very best to resolve the issues stemming from the aftermath of Gayle's not guilty verdict. No more shallow graves in the garden or other nocturnal visits. In fact, life for several months was pretty mundane. Perhaps routine has a cathartic rhythm that drives many demons away, or at least underground.

Kirsty developed other interests. Elliot helped. Children seem to master the abundance of fresh technology with ease. Another therapy, particularly for women, is shopping. After initial guidance, Kirsty entrenched herself into a plethora of retail websites; buying too much too often. Nobody complained. It was good to see her re-engaging with humdrum daily life.

In the quiet times, when nothing could hide it, she thought. There was the guilt. She had let Stephanie down, failed her. And around and around in her head, she tortured herself once again with the horrors she imagined her friend suffered, and the long lost remains that Craig Gayle had managed to conceal. Where to go? What to do? She was not giving up. Clearly, the legal system had achieved bugger all. The dogs had been called off. No policeman was interested in pursuing Gayle. Even her faithful, now neutered, officers had been sent back to the kennels. Despite a lingering gratitude, Warren Yates and Paul Leonard were dead in the water as far as she was concerned.

'All I get is junk,' Kirsty announced to her child tutor. 'If it's not companies trying to sell me rubbish, it's someone appealing for money.'

'Those sites you've been browsing and buying from keep your details or pass them on. Your email address is global now. You've got to expect anything and everything,' Elliot explained, attempting not to sound patronising.

'There's one here,' Kirsty groaned as she jabbed the screen of her tablet, 'that is asking me to support the return of capital punishment. Bring back hanging for murder and rape. What next?' For a moment, Kirsty allowed herself to visualise Craig Gayle, with tortured, crimson, squirming face, swinging, throttled by the gallows.

'Sell, persuade, recruit and activate. They are all out there,' Elliot informed his mother. 'Websites abound, and for every purpose. It's where the world raises issues, asks questions and highlights campaigns. There's no hiding from the online advocates and pressure groups.' Elliot was sounding a great deal older than his years. A child of the Internet.

His mother looked hard at the screen, yet didn't seem to be looking at it at all. Mesmerised, mouth hung open. Whizzing through the ring main of her brain were some crazy ideas and master plans of extraordinary complexity. 'How do they create a website, Elliot?' A slow, deliberate question. Steady voice, iron eyes.

'Why?' A kid's retort.

'How do they?' insisted Kirsty.

'Well, we do dabble a bit at school in ICT, but usually crappy stuff. I think there are companies that specialise in this sort of thing.' He hoped it was enough for his mother. Boredom was setting in.

Crusades have humble beginnings. Kirsty hunted the Net for ideas and strategy. A seed had been sown, and she saw crystal clear the whole new struggle that she would kick start. Tom would be furious. He thought she had put it to bed. Stephanie laid to rest. No, Kirsty wasn't forgetting the elephant in the room.

*

Dalton Riley had changed his name. It's something we all consider. Parents can be so short-sighted when it comes to handles for their offspring. Dalton needed to be cooler. He dressed Bayswater casual, colour flamboyant where needed, and skipped along with an off-the-shoulder cavalry bag for his tablet and iPhone; and the occasional packet of crisps. Kirsty had found his number after tapping meticulously into Google, searching for a local web page designer. He patted on the front door with his knuckles, musically. It was a habit, and avoided some ghastly chimes that came from poking a doorbell.

Formalities were pleasant and brief. Dalton was keen to make as much money as he could from this noticeably fragile woman. Reckoned she would buy all his various services. He envisaged quite a killing.

'What are we looking at here, Kirsty? I can call you Kirsty?' Dalton's face creased into a sickly smile as he lowered his trim buttocks to the sofa. Tight ankle-length trousers, sockless and scarlet Converse pumps. Legs gently crossed.

'Yes, that's fine,' Kirsty agreed. 'I simply want a page devoted to a friend who vanished a few years ago.' She was unsure about the dainty man pulling out his white iPad. 'Similar to those appeals that you see online.'

Dalton was quick to feel the cracks; a woman with little knowledge of the new technology and one he could manipulate. A vulnerability that he would feed off. 'Let's get some information.' A slimy grin as he confidently played at his keyboard.

Kirsty began. A saga of one sorely missed soul mate vanishing without trace, an interactive website that allowed those people who knew Stephanie to start conversations. She wasn't going to feed this dizzy kid with the details of Craig Gayle, of the trial and the outlandish verdict. Just for Stephanie. Pulling it all together. A lasting testament to her greatest friend. Posting photographs, swapping tales, fond memories; the significant and the silly. Stephanie never took herself seriously, so this should reflect her freewheeling nature. She spread it out for Dalton to sift through. Pick and mix.

'And dear,' Dalton swung his head and looked up, 'are you going to host this? Do you want your name floating around this website, or do you want this to be an anonymous gathering?'

Kirsty studied the floor, thinking it through. 'I think I want to be there. It needs someone as a catalyst.' Head raised proudly. Yes, she needed it known who she was and why this site was so special. 'I'm keen to be high profile here.'

'I will arrange some really inviting links, from the missing people groups to the lady's name and her geography. We will want yarns going back for yonks, won't we?' Dalton was on the case. It even surprised him how engaged he had become.

'I'll have something for you by next week, Kirsty,' Dalton assured her as he packed away his paraphernalia. 'In the meantime, I will need you to supply photographs and fill in some gaps in Stephanie's history. Expect an email with the connection so that you can scrutinize it all. Then let me know of any changes or errors; silly me occasionally mucks up, and I will adjust as necessary.' Dalton nearly skipped out towards the busy road. A flick of a wave as he cruised along the neck-high hedge. Quite a mission this one. Thinking and pickling ideas as he minced home.

True to his word, a classy *'For Stephanie'* website arrived the following week. Dalton Riley had surpassed himself. Kirsty was impressed. Disturbingly, Stephanie looked out at you bright-eyed and giggling. So alive, yet so very dead. Dalton had chosen carefully from the photos that Kirsty painfully parted with. Happy, carefree and bouncing from the page. Text that spoke of her bubbling generosity, her family, friends and her aspirations. With a plea from Kirsty to anyone who was directed to, or found the site, to ensure that her bosom buddy would not be forgotten. A request for past friends, colleagues, school chums and lovers to share anecdotes and events. And Kirsty's finally choking words about Stephanie's disappearance and the gaping hole in her life. Good font, layout inviting and graphics enticing. Quite the package.

Perhaps the most enterprising addition was the 'scribble wall'. Nothing new, but Dalton had grabbed a graphic of a rough red brick wall, like the side of a school building, where you could almost feel the grit and the coarseness, that site users could chalk on. Not unlike the side of the science lab that Stephanie leant against at break in her secondary establishment playground. Here site visitors were able to doodle messages, talk about their Stephanie recollections, update and post addresses for Kirsty to contact. It would be the place that Kirsty visited more than once a day. Checking in. Searching for something. Almost a shrine.

Slowly the scrawl, angled as if daubed in haste by a rascal

child, was left. Nothing much. Childhood tales and clouded memories, sun-baked street scenes, picnics, skirmishes and school outings. All positive and filled with some welcomed passion for Stephanie. Loved and lost. Gone but far from forgotten. And when there was more to say, Dalton had 'installed' a pathway to the pages of an exercise book where details could be added. A classroom atmosphere.

One frequent scribbler was Maureen Atkins. Changing room high jinks, teachers' nicknames, boys they both fancied and some illicit smoking. It seemed that when a memory flashed in her head, she sat at her computer and chalked it up. One particular event took longer, and into the book it went. A school ski trip. Some alcohol as they were in France, a ski instructor that all the girls took a shine to and an accident. According to the scrawled narrative of Maureen, Stephanie had acquired an indelible nickname following a crash with some babbling German at the end of a green run at the resort. Little Miss Bump. It was to stick until Stephanie left school.

An exciting rescue involving the handsome ski coach, a stretcher and all wrapped up for a winding journey to hospital. Apparently our Stephanie was badly injured. Two breaks, a clean fracture of the femur and a finger left dangling at a weird angle. Maureen, along with many of the girls, had visited her in the shabby-yet-cosy hospital. Experts on all injuries collected on the slopes. Stephanie's right leg was hung from some ceiling attachment, plaster from hip to calf. Ideal for drawn faces and silly comments. Stephanie enjoyed the celebrity but not the pain. It was a special flight back with a teacher a week after the rest of the party had left France. Kirsty even smiled at the thought of her friend stuck in hospital, ink-tattooed leg hanging from the roof.

Dalton wasn't exactly a computer genius, but he did employ some innovative ideas. The 'For Stephanie' website, connected to the scribble wall, accommodated access to a Facetime app. Maureen Atkins was determined to explore this device; some middle-aged women, kids flown, need a 'hobby'. Within days Kirsty was face to face with the gleeful smile of Maureen. Scarlet, puffed cheeks, and bulbous eyes that were seemingly laser incisive. It took time for the two women to grasp the notion of swaying faces and online voices. It was Kirsty who spoke first.

'If you put your iPad on a stand, you won't keep tottering about.'

'Sorry, not used to this thing,' Maureen muttered, as she continued to wobble on the screen.

Kirsty tried her best not to spy on her own image that hung in a small square screen, top right of the main one. Didn't want to look at the darkening eye bags, the frown lines that wrinkled her forehead, her haunted face.

'Have you read all my comments about Stephanie?' asked Maureen.

'Yes, you had a lot to say,' Kirsty tried to politely answer.

'Our Little Miss Bump. That was a trip,' Maureen spluttered. 'Steph really smashed herself up. And, did I tell you about the trouble she had after that?'

'Trouble, what trouble?'

'Well,' Maureen began, and shuffled in her seat, head swaying on the screen, 'Our Little Miss Bump was the hell to travel with. There were other school journeys, and every time we were going through security, Steph set off the alarms. It was chaos.'

'Set off the alarms, why?' Kirsty enquired.

'Well, you see, when they repaired her injuries from the skiing accident, they inserted metal rods. One in the top of her leg and one, a small one, in her finger. The metal instantly alerted the scanner, and there she blows. Every time. After the first few sirens, poor Steph had to carry a letter confirming to airport staff the origin of the steel rod in her leg.'

Maureen Atkins continued to list events and episodes, but Kirsty couldn't rid herself of the metal rods that had been used to heal her friend. Kept rustling it through her head, kept hold of it as if there were some importance in this revelation. As soon as she could, she shook off Maureen, promising to catch up later and perhaps swap further stories.

Nicholas Gayle wasn't around much following the trial, and Kirsty hadn't seen him for some time. However, she was keen to corner the lad. The metal rods. Nicholas would know, wouldn't he? He was the only one she could approach. Since the not guilty verdict and Nicholas's reluctance to testify, he and Kirsty hadn't spoken. Now she needed to urgently. She manufactured a text message that she thought would winkle him out. And waited. It was a day before a feeble reply pinged back. Tea at her house, like old times, a chat no more. No recriminations or grumbled disappointments. Nicholas was 'popping in' the next day.

'Metal rods?' Nicholas mumbled.

'Yes, your mum had these to help heal her broken bones,' Kirsty explained. 'As a girl skiing with the school. A friend has confirmed this.'

'So?' Nicholas could see no point in the subject. 'It happens when people break bones. Anyway, I sort of knew there was something. Mum didn't give us the whole story, but when we flew she was always holding us up at airport security.'

'Why was that?' Kirsty edged closer.

'The alarms were constantly going off. She would take off her shoes, jewellery and belt; and end up only half-dressed. It must have been those metal rods that were setting things off. She didn't tell us.' Nicholas sat back in the sofa rubbing his chin, thinking about those times.

Kirsty's head buzzed. So many thoughts and ideas, but now they were a random mess. She would be all right in the morning.

Chapter Fifteen

And in the morning, the glittering water of Island Barn Reservoir was giving up its dead.

In the midst of a carpet of floating gulls, disturbance. The birds were jumbled, squawking and arcing towards land, away from the intrusion. Breaking the glassy water at that point, having slipped from its shackles and risen from the depths, a once blue tarpaulin bundle, tubular, bobbed and sank only to bob again.

Island Barn Reservoir boasts a vibrant sailing club, and a young group of would-be mariners were tacking their way across the rippling water. Sailing is a skill not easily learned, and the wicked boom was swinging wildly in the boat filled with excited voices when the fibreglass bow hit the bobbing object. A dull thud, no more. Curious faces could only make out the stringy weed and patterned sediment that adorned the canvas lump. It was treasure. They were out in a sailing boat and had found a fortune. It was like one of the books they had read. But this was a long way from Enid Blyton. Desperate attempts to tow the mucky bale failed, and it wasn't until Captain Williams (retired), in charge of operations on the reservoir, was hailed that there were serious efforts to capture the bundle.

It was too much like a dead body not to be one. Captain Williams summoned the police and left the roped tarpaulin parcel to bobble at the quayside. A cursory inspection by the local rooky plod, which entailed prodding it with a stick and taking a snap, warranted a higher authority. It wasn't an emergency. A desk sergeant scribbled down essentials and locations. Some young Bobbies would be enough of a cavalry. And as the paperwork trundled through the station system, a busy woman who thought she knew it all recognised some details from the Gayle case. She made sure, with a smug smile, that Inspector Warren Yates and Sergeant Paul Leonard, crouched in their hutch, were aware. Stephanie? This was a warmer case than the other historic paperwork they needed to sift through. Despite the dire warnings of Collins-Maynard, the two men were off.

Yates and Leonard arrived at the wooden landing stage soon after the young officers who had been officially sent. The tarpaulin package had already been hauled onto the rough timber dock, water draining through the gaps in the planks. Perhaps the braver of the two policemen knelt down to preliminary inspect it and test the strength of the ropes that knotted it secure. He decided on a more direct approach, pulled a penknife from his pocket and started to saw at the twine. The tarpaulin flapped open at one end. Feet. Well, they had been feet. Bones of feet and some stringy skin holding on in places. Brave as he might have thought he was, the young policeman stood quickly upright. Face ashen, lips quivering. The splutter of vomit.

'Forensics,' Warren Yates demanded. An audience, midst whisper, stepped back a pace. Scientists were called.

It didn't take long for the agitated scrum of a white-robed forensic team to busy themselves at the reservoir. Photographs of everything, tarpaulin eased open, a rotting corpse, face down, matted dark hair, protruding skeleton, the fishbone pattern of a putrid ribcage. Could easily be Stephanie, thought Inspector Yates. Paul Leonard needed to see more, desperate to turn the body over, to see what was left of the facial features. No chance. The cadaver, once fully examined and photographed from all angles in situ, was trundled off to the mortuary.

Two sharpen-minded policemen now watched as the paraphernalia of a scientific investigation were loaded and driven away. Two pondering policemen thinking hard about their next move. Warren Yates spoke first, 'We are less than a mile from Kirsty's house.'

'Yeah,' Paul Leonard sighed, 'less than a mile from Craig Gayle's home.' They exchanged knowing glances. 'Would only be good sense to talk to Kirsty again, update her and explore possibilities.'

'Much like what I had in mind,' Inspector Yates mumbled, chewing over the facts.

Kirsty stepped back at the arrival of the two officers, but they were received as old friends and were quickly offered tea. As she shuffled biscuits onto a plate, she pried. 'Good to see you both; to what do I owe this honour?'

Warren Yates, aware of his now unofficial status, kept his head low, stooped. As if talking to his shoes. 'You know Island Barn Reservoir just up the road?'

'Yes.' Kirsty was intrigued but yet to grasp the direction of this enquiry.

'We have found... floating... from the depths,' Warren continued awkwardly, 'a body.'

Kirsty was on it immediately, on her feet. 'Stephanie? Have you found Stephanie?'

'Unsure. We haven't been able to really identify the corpse yet,' added Paul Leonard.

'It must be.' Eagerness in Kirsty's voice. 'That bastard Gayle must've dumped her there.' She was seething now.

'We'll know soon. Once the pathologists have fully examined and carried out tests, we will have answers,' Paul carefully explained. He wasn't going to describe the rotting corpse that he had seen. If it was Stephanie, it was nothing like her now. It was nothing like any human. Death is indiscriminate and reduces the most beautiful to a horrific tangle of what had once made up the perfect structure. Once again, Gayle was in his sights.

When the kids had gone to bed and Tom was in the study, Kirsty slipped out. It was a short walk to the reservoir, and as she ambled along she pictured Craig Gayle carrying Stephanie's lifeless body along the same track she was using. A motionless lump that had been her beautiful friend, simply being disposed of, like a sack of rubbish. Kirsty wiped a trickling tear spreading across her cheek.

It was probably trespassing, but she had to be there. The boathouse security lights sprang on as she turned the corner. Hopefully, there would be no cameras. Kirsty's shoes clattered on the boards of the wooden jetty. The security lights went out behind her. Darkness. Some birds fluttered nearby, climbed with thrashing wings, probably gulls. A pale moon flitted between clouds, and with each passing spread a blue light across the placid expanse of water. Just dumped there. Perhaps wrapped up and weighted down. Lovely Stephanie. Kirsty reached for the water as if it was some ceremony for her lost friend, as if it was some connection, some closure. She stayed swirling the water with flicking fingers, running through her head some of those moments when Stephanie was so alive, so full of fun and energy. It must have been an hour. It didn't matter.

Chapter Sixteen

The Croydon Public Mortuary, the nearest one to Island Barn, had previously been steeped in its Victorian past, heavily tiled, body cabinets dented and on the edge of rusting. Now, courtesy of a makeover, it was crystal transparent, with glass walls, clinically Spartan and an array of stainless steel slabs and storage, ready to welcome the constant flow of cadavers. Putting a great number of hospitals to shame. The dead deserved this.

On a central stainless steel tray, remaining face down, still clothed in the faded blue tarpaulin, hanging twine and rotting dead. Stephanie was beyond dead. Each move would be recorded, every item of clothing listed, and all body parts carefully arranged. Reginald Cadwallader, the respected forensic pathologist, hovered over the remains. A lay person would not know where to start; a lay person would probably be dangling a contorted bunch of their guts and ready to pass out. Reginald had seen it all before and began efficiently. He knew this would take a long time. He also knew the two policemen, rambling around the viewing room, would want him to be quick.

In particular, Warren Yates wanted identity. If this was Stephanie, he would be looking for further clues and evidence to hang on Craig Gayle. He and Paul Leonard would have to be patient and watch the bulky figure of Reginald Cadwallader use all sorts of equipment to examine this body. It would take hours before it could be turned, before the policemen would be able to see what was left of Stephanie Gayle's face. What was left of Stephanie Gayle. It was obvious mid-afternoon that Cadwallader was taking his time, and the two officers decided to leave and return early the next day. Neither had the stomach to eat much that evening.

By the time they arrived in Croydon the following day, Cadwallader and his team had organised well. Items of clothing were laid on one table, the tarpaulin (strings attached) on another. A body laid out orderly. Bones in their place. Static, face down.

'About to reveal the frontal section,' announced Reginald Cadwallader over the speaker system. The mortuary team knew their places and how the process progressed. Stephanie was eased over. Some body parts were reluctant, some detaching, and the procedure was, at times, messy. Although they couldn't hear it, the two policemen sensed it rattled or splattered into place. Cadwallader was down quickly; touching nothing, he observed from all sides and stood back, rubbing his chin. 'Can't be certain, but this looks like it isn't the female you expected. Afraid it's a bloke. Even all that time in the water hasn't completely destroyed his genitalia. Sorry.'

'Shit!' exclaimed Warren Yates.

'Holy Moses,' Paul Leonard added politely.

'If it isn't Stephanie, who is it?' quizzed Warren. 'Who the fuck has been rotting at the bottom of a fucking reservoir?' He was puzzled yet obviously disappointed. When you visualise the end of the road only to find you have another journey ahead, it leaves you like this. He slumped in a chair.

On the slab was the distorted, buck-toothed, sunken head. Dark caves where there had been eyes, a nose of hanging gristle and barely any flesh at the cheeks. 'A dark-haired individual, male as I have said, fine clothing and in his twenties, average height by the look of it. No apparent causes of death. Complex examinations to do. Skin too shredded to indicate damage there.' Cadwallader was up with the policemen giving a brief summary of the post-mortem so far. 'When we have the test results and toxicology report back, we should know more.'

'Any evidence to identify this stiff?' Warren enquired, no longer with the politeness offered to the departed when he thought it was Stephanie.

'Nothing. No names in the clothing. Tarpaulin could be a clue,' Cadwallader muttered.

Kirsty had to be told. Paul Leonard was ushered round to the Foster home. She was waiting, expecting news of Stephanie's death; gruesome stuff but maybe confirmation that Craig Gayle couldn't escape from. Something that would definitely nail him. Paul was hailed in.

Kirsty waited in silence. Paul's head was bent as he spoke. Thank you, Inspector Yates, he thought, for making me convey the news. 'It's not Stephanie.' Brief and to the point.

'What?' Kirsty reeled back. 'Not Stephanie. You mean that was not Stephanie in the water?' She slumped on the sofa, disappointed, disappointed that this wasn't her friend, and that would mean closure. Somewhere inside she held on to the precarious lifeline that Stephanie was still alive. A little embarrassed now about her trip to the reservoir the previous night. 'Who is it?' she managed.

'No identity yet,' Paul explained. 'They'll be piecing things together at the morgue. Could be a while before we have anything.'

Back in Croydon, the autopsy team busied themselves with

the meticulous task of finding out who the rotting body belonged to and possibly how he had died. Clothing went one way, stomach contents another, organs tested and dissected, DNA laboratory bound, and every inch of this cadaver examined. Team work. Reginald Cadwallader had the best.

Chapter Seventeen

Reginald Cadwallader stood with his thumbs hooked in his check waistcoat pockets, nose in the air. Something of Toad of Toad Hall arrogance about his stance. Assembled were his staff, Warren Yates and Paul Leonard. Two policemen who were now lacking their original enthusiasm when they thought the rotting body from Island Barn Reservoir was that of Stephanie Gayle, brutally murdered by her arsehole husband. Cadwallader was ready to pronounce his findings. On stage. He loved an audience.

'Male, five foot seven inches. Late twenties, early thirties. He wasn't drowned, no water in his lungs. He had been throttled; most probably with a heavy rope or cable. Enough to break his neck. Vertebra snapped. Usually happens when the killer attacks his victim from behind.' Cadwallader pulled violently at an imaginary strangling cord as if he were the murderer. 'Been dead for around ten months, maybe longer. This cold water slows down the decaying process. From my examination of his clothes, I would suggest he was a foreign man. Most likely a European. Some skin slivers that could be examined closely implied the same. No idea yet as to his identity. Missing persons have been studied, and an attempted DNA match made. No success. I have sent samples to our European colleagues at the Paris centre. We appear to have access to this service for now.' Cadwallader waited for questions. There were none.

This was now a fresh homicide inquiry. Yates and Leonard slid away, knowing some younger, smart-arsed detectives, brimming with enthusiasm, would soon be churning through the case. Nothing for Yates and Leonard. They headed back to their small room at Wimbledon nick. A little too premature.

Cadwallader studied his notes, lifted his glasses and continued. 'Perhaps helpful to the enquiry is that the body was wrapped and tied with materials you would associate with commercial use. Heavy canvas that sellers use to cover barrows and stalls at night, and coarse rope used to secure these sheets. A blue tarpaulin that retained evidence of white advertisement printing. If this had been clearer we could have been sure of its origin. Nothing legible was apparent.' Warren Yates and Paul Leonard should have stayed. It wasn't until they read the written report several days later that they were alerted. Yates, even in the autumn of his career, didn't believe in coincidences.

'Paul, get on to that Europol mate of yours in France. I know Cadwallader is chasing the DNA on this, but I need to hurry this up. I smell a rat here.' Warren Yates was tasting action again. He closed another beige cold-case file he had been yawning over and stood to think. Standing was important to jolt a slowing brain.

'What exactly are we looking for?' Paul Leonard queried. 'Won't Cadwallader's feelers be enough?'

'It's in the guts. It's always been in my guts. There's something we are not seeing here. I need that identification quick, bloody quick.' Warren's nose was to the ground. 'Less than a mile from Gayle's house. Easy to reach that reservoir. Materials from perhaps a market. There's a link. Not sure of it yet, but I bloody will soon. It may not be the body of Stephanie. If Gayle's a killer, then he may not have stopped there.'

Kirsty was a mother and a wife. She was back behaving like one. Holding on to her folders of thought, but keeping its distance, was the disappointing reservoir find. Warren Yates phoned her. He summarised what Cadwallader had announced about the corpse and prodded her for ideas as to the origin of the tarpaulin. Had she seen anything like that lying around the Gayle property? Is this stuff he could have got his hands on? Any association would help. Who could he have murdered? If it was him? Just when things were following a steady path, along comes this diversion. She would think about it and get back to Yates. Nothing and nobody had come to mind.

'Murder squad are down at the reservoir. Divers, submergible cameras, scanners, the works. Maybe they'll find other bodies. It's deep, frighteningly deep.' Paul Leonard hated water, especially deep water. Something threatening about the blackened depths, man-contained, cold. He shuddered.

'Bound to happen. One squalid carcass we know about. Island Barn Reservoir could be guarding a graveyard down there. Maybe strewn with a host of bodies. Perhaps Stephanie is rotting deep in the water. Just one of the decaying corpses littering the floor.' Warren Yates would wait. 'Just tell those DCs to keep us updated,' Yates instructed his sergeant.

Kirsty wasn't at her computer as much. A few words about the body in Island Barn and a brief update from Maureen Atkins about Stephanie's skiing disaster. Otherwise 'the wall' was receiving little attention despite a few enquiries about other secrets the reservoir might hold. Quiet times. When you have been a regular visitor to online pages, it's more habit that takes you there than reason. Kirsty scrolled through the early history when there were many people scrawling and absorbing memories of her friend, until the entries faded to almost nothing... except, an easily missed note in a high corner of the page, loitering near the top of the wall. As if jotted in embarrassment. *'Feeling the guilt, Dean'*.

Feeling the guilt? What does that mean? Kirsty thought to herself.

There was no way of knowing the writer. Anonymity. Dalton had designed it like that. Freedom to scrawl would lead more people to the wall. Let them open up and feed the page incognito if they wanted. It would appear that Dean surely wanted just that. Kirsty would watch a little more closely over the next few days. She was up for grasping straws.

The divers and the dredgers took a couple of weeks to scour the bottom of the reservoir and haul up nothing more than some old bikes, pushchairs and an assortment of domestic litter. No more bodies. Paul Leonard's phone rang in the cramped office at Wimbledon. It was his friend at Europol. They had located what they believed to be a DNA match with the sample Cadwallader had sent. Deep in Europe, a family member who was recently arrested for a drug offence was on the register, which could lead to the identification of the mystery cadaver. They were pursuing this lead. Would be in touch shortly. True to their word, a call came through later that day. Paul Leonard was stuck statue-like holding the telephone receiver, eyes wide, unblinking.

Chapter Eighteen

'Demetrio Natano. The fucking body they hauled out of the reservoir was most probably our Portuguese lover, Demetrio Natano.' Paul Leonard was gobsmacked.

Warren Yates doesn't move quickly. It's the slowness of experience and age. However, this time he was on his feet like a gymnast. 'Fuck me, I don't believe it. Demetrio Natano at the bottom of a reservoir, murdered.' Warren gawped at nothing. 'Where are we going now?' A whole new enquiry and a whirlwind of fancies.

'Appears a brother was apprehended just outside Lisbon. DNA on record and apparently easy to match the sample Cadwallader had sent Europol. They didn't have Demetrio documented, but there was no doubting the family fit. This has opened a can of worms.' Paul Leonard sagged into his chair. Both men incubating their silence; thrown adrift by this new evidence, brains buzzing with all manner of notions.

'Didn't he make his way back to Portugal when Gayle was awaiting trial? That was the general belief at the time,' Warren Yates thought aloud. 'No one could find him to attend court, and it was common knowledge he'd done a runner. Well, it would appear he didn't. The poor fellow wasn't running anywhere. Now, who made sure of that? One thing for certain, we don't want the media getting hold of this. No one breathes a word to the papers, and we must make sure Cadwallader remains stumm.'

'More than just a finger points to our likely lad, Craig Gayle,' Paul Leonard pronounced.

'Yep.' Yates was on the phone straight away. 'Hello, Chief Superintendent Collins-Maynard, please.' This case was thrown wide open, and Warren Yates wasn't going to lose his man again.

'Yes?' the superintendent barked down the mouthpiece. It wasn't that long ago that he had slung these two idiots out of his office after they had bungled the Gayle trial and wasted the force a great deal of money and police time. 'What exactly, Inspector Yates, do you want with me? And it better not be another of your wild goose chases. I'm not paying for you to piss about with a cold case dead end.'

Warren Yates trod carefully; the old man was fuming, and he could picture the crimson cheeks of the Superintendent ready to explode big time. 'If you remember, of course you do, the disappearance of Stephanie Gayle, well, there has been a dramatic discovery, a breakthrough, that warrants further investigation.'

Seething and spitting out his words, the superintendent clutched the phone. 'I told you, this department cannot plough money into any more of your fanciful ideas or leads, which lead nowhere. I am only interested in watertight evidence and airtight confidence to bring a successful prosecution. You can go and sing elsewhere this time.' Collins-Maynard was an old duffer, and he intended to be a really huge old duffer today.

'A body was recovered from the reservoir close to the Gayle house.' Warren was determined the superintendent heard him out. 'This radically affects this case, and it isn't anything the press would consider the national police force should ignore. Don't you think? Wouldn't want the paparazzi to haul you through their pages, would you?'

There was some considerable huffing and puffing from Collins-Maynard and then the hiss of expelling air. 'So you've found her; Stephanie Gayle's body has been recovered from a local reservoir? It's news that should conclude the case. Well done.' Collins-Maynard offered reluctant congratulations to his inspector.

Warren took a deep breath. 'Unfortunately, the body salvaged from the water was not that of Stephanie Gayle.' Well aware of how the superintendent would react to this news, he was quick to continue. 'It has, however, now been identified as that of Demetrio Natano. If you recall, this was the young Portuguese man who was sexually implicated with Craig Gayle and Steve Bairstow, a no-show prosecution witness in Gayle's murder trial. It had been assumed that Natano fled to his native Portugal to avoid being called to testify. Apparently, someone decided it was far better to permanently prevent such a witness appearance.'

'Not Stephanie Gayle? I was under the impression that your news was going to secure a conviction here with the discovery of the corpse, not find some peripheral figure that might well just stretch this case out further but arrive nowhere. You want me to okay an additional period of police expenditure on another whim?'

'Let Sergeant Leonard and me deal with it. I am not expecting the cavalry, just agree that this case still has the legs to continue. No more money or staffing. We'll do it all.' Warren Yates was holding out an olive branch.

'Okay, okay. You two can try and revive this one on your own. Keep me updated. You are well aware it would take an earth movement to get Gayle back to court. I am certain that I am not being called a dick again.' Collins-Maynard slammed the telephone receiver down and muttered his way to the toilet. The strong diuretic he had recently been prescribed was playing havoc with his bladder.

'Paul, we are on our own. There is going to be no help from outside. The chief super thinks we are barking up the wrong tree again. I'm sure there's a trail here that we can follow. Keep close, share information, and discuss options. We'll be all right.' Warren Yates was sounding like a competent detective. 'What exactly have we got? I need to plan this out carefully. The superintendent thinks we are tumbling down another cul-de-sac. I intend to show him he's wrong.'

'Steve Bairstow is a suspect,' Paul Leonard began, 'but there's more evidence, although some is circumstantial, that Gayle chose this option to muzzle his lover. Bairstow was fuming about how Gayle had stolen the Portuguese nancy boy when they had their own cosy arrangement. There's a chance his revenge was to take Demetrio out; what he couldn't have, he was certain Craig Gayle wasn't going to have. There would be some satisfaction knowing that Gayle would suffer.'

Warren Yates' head swayed, and he sucked in his bottom lip. 'Bairstow could have deliberately dumped the body near Gayle's home and used materials from the market that would implicate him. Possible. What we mustn't do is attempt to fit all our evidence into a scenario that suits us, suits Collins-Maynard, and keeps the investigation tidy. Open minds, Paul, open minds.'

'If I were Craig Gayle and had murdered my wife, and perhaps divulged inner secrets to my new love during passionate engagement, I would be certain to gag him. That's why we thought he had made sure the guy was whizzed back to

Portugal at the time of the trial. Could be we were wrong, and instead, he silenced him for good. You don't want to drag a body about any distance, and that reservoir is an easy dumping ground for Gayle.' Paul Leonard scratched his neck and looked aimlessly around him. 'We are going to have to tread carefully here. I suggest we have a word with Kirsty Foster. She needs to know. When she discovered it wasn't Stephanie they had hauled from the water, events had battered her again. Perhaps there's a way to the truth here.'

'Cup of tea?' offered Kirsty as the two policemen called round, faces stuck smiling, at the door. 'Here on business or just passing?' Kirsty slipped into the kitchen.

'A bit of both,' Warren called from the lounge. He didn't sit, just wandered around the room looking at, but not really taking notice of, family photos propped on the side and hung in frames. Fading ones of her and Stephanie now arranged to form a frontage.

Paul and Warren sank into the sagging sofa when Kirsty brought the tea and some unexciting biscuits. 'Well?' she asked. 'Not much happening this end. Have you news?'

'We have an identification of the body they found in Island Barn Reservoir. We had all thought that this was Stephanie. As you know, it wasn't. It was male. A rotting man in rough tarpaulin. He'd been killed and dumped there. There was a general sigh of disappointment. We now have an identity. What it all means remains a puzzle. There are jigsaw pieces, but they don't yet fit together.' Warren Yates was circling in, ready to shock. 'There's a connection. It was, Kirsty, the body of our Portuguese queer, Demetrio Natano. That sodden corpse thrown up from the depths of the reservoir was Craig Gayle's lover boy, Demetrio.'

Kirsty strained forward in her armchair. 'Him?' She was unsure of the significance, unsure of what it meant to her whole crusade. 'Who murdered this one?' She covered her face with clammy hands. Stephanie's fate whizzed through her thoughts. Knew the likelihood that her friend had received the same treatment, that her body was wasting away in some other grave, water or soil. 'Gayle?'

'We're progressing carefully. Gayle has already escaped us, jumped through hoops at the trial, and the force is not going to pursue the guy without justification. We'll do all we can to solve this, along with help from some novice murder squad detectives. As Paul and I see it, there are only two possible contenders for this killing, Gayle and Steve Bairstow.' Detective Inspector Yates attempted to sound hopeful.

Chapter Nineteen

Yates and Leonard didn't stay around for long. They were hounds with a scent and scampered off in pursuit. Kirsty found solace at her computer. At Stephanie's wall, she thought about writing something about Demetrio's body being found in the reservoir, but was unsure if it sensationalised Stephanie's disappearance. As usual, scrawled in one corner was a further note from Dean; he wasn't sleeping well, *nightmares*. What's he on about? Where does he fit in? Kirsty thought. She would keep an eye out. Maybe this Dean had something to do with Stephanie's disappearance. Very often murderers don't work alone. Some ugly thoughts were swimming in her head. A glass of wine might well disperse them. In part, it did.

Dean Wallace was a loner. Probably autistic. He had struggled through school and had never held down a permanent job. A man who could work with his hands, but that was about that. Even decisions were a trial for his labouring brain. In his one-bedroom housing association home, he muddled through a simple life. Nothing demanding; he liked that. Coping without extending. It was perhaps for the better that no one shared his middle age. Men like Dean take a long time jumbling through their thoughts. He had decided to contact Kirsty Foster after some agonising hours retrieving some puzzling history. It was about the time of Stephanie's disappearance. Highlighted by the Daily Mail's coverage of Craig Gayle's trial, the defendant's mug sneering from the front page. He knew that face. At that time he had been working at a job not at all challenging once he'd learned the routine. Dean was a man who could manage procedures that were predictable. He was also a man who could be trampled over, misused and abused. Easy pickings.

Kirsty wrote on her own wall. It was the only way to reach this Dean character. He was probably a creepy online loser. Some irritant who poked around Internet sites looking to play games at other people's expense. A neutered troll. She prodded for further information, some contact, perhaps a chat.

*

Warren Yates spread out photographs that filled his desk top. Some slid to the floor. He sighed in a way that those nearing pension age sighed, as it appeared that the floor was moving further away from him daily. In transparent bags were clothes, tarpaulin and rope, well more of a twine. 'Paul, if you work on this baggage or packaging, I'll try and create a time line for this guy's movements and more details on how he snuffed it. Of course, we are looking for a link with Gayle or Bairstow.' Warren Yates had taken charge. Nose to the ground.

'Have forensic finished with this stuff?' Paul questioned before he threw the bags onto his own desk.

'You don't get much from clothes and canvas when it's been languishing under water for months. There's some hope that they've salvaged something from the lashing that held the tarpaulin together. Twisted rope often captures and withholds evidence that smoother surfaces lose. So, some prospect there.' Warren wanted to, but didn't, sound that hopeful.

*

Kirsty's schedule settled. Children were sent to school, taken to activities, and fed. Tom commuted now; a steady desk job in the City. He too was following a routine, although to him it felt more like a rut. When you have flitted amidst oilfields in remarkable locations, it was painful now to be piling into the steamy carriages to fight for a journey to the Big Smoke. And in the peace of the day, Kirsty found comfort at her computer. Dean was in her head, and she needed to track him down; she was left with long shots. Some early exchange was established, followed by friendly massaging words. Dean wanted to talk, as if there was something to unburden. But he'd fallen off the radar. No recent visits to the wall. Kirsty was cautious; you don't just invite strangers round to your home. She would speak to him but held out little hope that this was going anywhere. Tom would have to be roped in, despite his reluctance to dabble in what he regarded as a lost cause. Dead in the water. High-profile spot with Tom nearby. Her plan was doomed to fail. Our Dean was in a little trouble.

Dean Wallace was now being entertained. Unfortunately, it was at 'Her Majesty's Pleasure'. Locked up in Pentonville. Even avoiding conviction was difficult for Dean. Serving nearly three years for dealing in stolen property. Men like Dean lack the sharpness to succeed in such business. Dull-witted and without the ability to negotiate the system and avoid some obvious traps; Dean had been well trapped, caught red-handed and easily sent down. Police enjoy dealing with such simple rogues.

Being inside, banged up, gives you time to think. And thinking was something that Dean Wallace found difficult. However, he had managed to persuade a petty criminal, who was about to be released, to 'nail' a note on Stephanie's wall for him, making readers aware of his detention; he'd been taken for a fool, and even a social misfit doesn't like being used.

Kirsty discovered Dean's misfortune late in the evening. Never mind, she thought, probably a red herring, going nowhere. She would concentrate on digging up other leads. She wasn't a woman who was stalled by a hurdle. And this Dean guy would be out soon. She decided to let Warren Yates know the next morning.

*

'We've got Gayle's DNA from his previous arrest; when we have results back we need to check for a match. In the meantime, get down the market and swab that guy Bairstow. Those are the only leads we have. No other obvious suspects.' Inspector Warren Yates briefed his assistant. Paul Leonard shrugged and nodded. He was aware there was scant hope of progress.

'Fancy a holiday, Paul?' Warren Yates asked, his face holding a grin.

'Holiday? You've just asked me to hunt down DNA, and now you're suggesting it's vacation time.' Paul was puzzled.

'We need to explore Demetrio's Portuguese base. His family and friends. There may be something there that we're missing. Could be he'd been blabbing over there,' Warren added. 'So off you go to the sun. Have fun.'

Paul Leonard shrugged; an order was an order, but he wasn't sure this was going anywhere.

*

Warren Yates took Kirsty's call. 'You say he's locked up, Kirsty?'

'Yes, I know it's probably a blind alley, but I'm grasping at straws. Dean's the name, and I'll send you the scrawled messages I've been getting. You have a look and get back to me, Inspector, all right?' Kirsty could detect a polite indifference. Warren Yates was a people pleaser but found it difficult to hide his lack of enthusiasm.

Dean Wallace wasn't hard to find. Police data records are amazingly reliable, and Warren Yates was astonished at how quickly he located his Dean. Pentonville, two years nine months. A regular. Yates wouldn't haul him out and shake him down at the station or in a solitary interrogation room at the prison. No, he would go during visiting. Less attention drawn.

Pentonville; the name makes you imagine an American new town or care home. However, HMP Pentonville is a London category B prison, overcrowded, bristling with experienced convicts and a spattering of habitual minor-league offenders. Sinister Victorian grey, a greyness copied by neighbouring housing, and an uninterrupted gloom that lingered over this backwater of London. As with all similar institutions, there was a dark hierarchy of inmates and a sloppy army of prison warders. One group had the power, and the other thought they had. Any new prisoner soon became aware of whom to obey, what to say and when. An overlord by the name of Buggy ruled Pentonville. He watched over the visitor hall, and in particular, at the antics of Dean Wallace as he was brought to his dubious interrogator. Warren Yates was Old Bill, and Buggy was ensuring no 'in-house' stuff was discussed. He had an empire to defend.

Old and cold, high and unwelcoming, a meeting gallery where you faced your family, grim-faced adults and confused kids. Formica tables and heavy footsteps; the drifting stench of prison food. A filing in of bloated inmates, dour faces. Dean Wallace, wily, nervous and lightly shuffling; as if mentally challenged, hunched, eyes springing each way, darting between inmates and visitors. Warren Yates clocked him straight away. Dean was yet to meet his rare visitor. He fumbled with his grey institutional tracksuit top.

'Dean Wallace?' Warren approached the pathetic figure and guided him to a table far from the scrum of other visitors and their old lags. 'How are you?' Of course, Dean wasn't the happiest human on the planet. A police inspector has to begin with a sense of compassion despite what might follow. Trundling between families and prison warders, a pleasant chubby woman was dishing out beverages and biscuits. Warren hailed her over and grabbed two mugs of tea and a chipped plate strewn with dark brown bourbon pieces that resembled a broken Jenga game.

Through slurping sips, Inspector Warren Yates began. 'It seems that you have been contacting people on the Internet, Dean?'

'Wha'd' you mean?' An immediate defensive response from the sad convict.

'Nothing dodgy, Dean; it's not like we are following your porn site visits. I am not here to discuss any aspect of your personal life or accuse you of wrong doing. No, it's quite a harmless enquiry.' Warren smiled broadly; he was putting the irritated man at ease.

'A very pleasant lady by the name of Kirsty Foster tells me you've contacted her, or should I say the website that she supervises. Apparently, you write on a digital wall, a sort of casual way of swapping information.' Warren Yates slumped back in his chair in an attempt to appear relaxed and to put Dean at ease.

'Yeah, I did that. Something been bothering me a while,' Dean blurted. 'I seen in the papers when that guy was on trial. You know, the one where 'is missus went missing. They thought they'd bang him up for that. Kept an eye on 'ow it went. He got away wiv it, you know?'

'You think he did it then? You're convinced that Stephanie Gayle was killed by her husband, Craig, and that he has kept the secret of her disappearance and that of her body?' Warren pushed himself forward and engaged his policeman's voice. 'What makes you certain of his guilt?'

'That's why I wrote on the website. It was about the time, if I've got it right, that she went missing. It's bugged me ever since. Always had my suspicions. That fucking man done it all right. Now listen to this.' Dean had his elbows further across the table, encroaching on Warren's space. His face had reddened and his glassy eyes were unblinking. 'Ain't much of a brain box, me. Do what I can. Nothing I really have to think about. Jobs, I mean. Use me 'ands not me 'ead. And I've had a lot of 'em, dead-end jobs.' Dean smirked, a joke made by mistake. 'Don't seem to last long. Well, this dead-end job' – Dean gurgled something reminiscent of a chuckle – 'was where it all 'appened.'

Prison visiting periods don't last long. Many families had already left. Warren Yates hadn't even started. Perhaps he had spent too long loosening Dean Wallace; making him malleable. Warders, jangling bunches of keys, ushered the last remaining visitors through swinging double doors. They knew who stayed.

No questions. Warren and Dean were alone in the echoing room. Buggy had his suspicions and loitered nearby.

'You are telling me, Dean, that you know what happened to Stephanie Gayle?' Warren Yates was more policeman now. 'I am all ears.'

'I think I do, and it ain't no bullshit. It weren't me. What I can tell you don't mean I were involved.' Dean drew a deep breath.

Chapter Twenty

Chief Superintendent Collins-Maynard was not going to like it. Paul Leonard was attempting to draw together a bunch of loose ends in the Demetrio Natano unlawful killing case. If clues do come in bunches, this bunch wasn't holding together well. With Warren Yates chasing phantoms at Pentonville prison, he was holding fort and expecting the chief superintendent very soon. Collins-Maynard arrived with a crash. His expansive body burst through the door of the small office where Paul Leonard was laying out his ware.

'I haven't got much time, Detective,' the superintendent muttered as he plonked himself onto a rather unsteady chair next to Paul Leonard's cluttered desk. 'What have you to offer? You know how I feel about this bloody business, and this death is a deflecting spin-off of that thorny cold case that you and Yates have been bungling for some time.'

'Demetrio Natano, Portuguese, worked at the New Covent Garden Market with two figures closely involved in the Stephanie Gayle disappearance. In a homosexual relationship with both Steve Bairstow and Craig Gayle. Went missing at the time of the Gayle trial; assumed he'd fled back to his native Portugal to avoid questioning.' Paul Leonard stopped to consult his clipboard. 'His body floated to the surface of Island Barn Reservoir, which is barely a mile away from the Gayle home. We had hoped this was a conclusion to Stephanie's disappearance; that our corpse was that of Mrs Gayle. Sadly no.

Natano had, they roughly determine, been in that deep water for ten months. His badly decomposed remains ensured that the cause of death was difficult to determine and the perpetrator even more difficult to identify.' Collins-Maynard shifted irritated on the creaking chair. Fingers drumming a wobbly table. He knew most of the background that he was hearing. He wasn't a patient man. Paul Leonard recognised this.

'To move forward quickly, as I know you are in a hurry, here are the details of our investigation into the reservoir body and the matter of its concealment. The deceased man was a mess. Not mess enough to foil our master-solver of a cadaver problem, Reginald Cadwallader. Throttled, neck broken, vertebrae dislodged. A violent killing by a violent assailant. Wrapped in the funeral garb of a London market, a worn and grubby tarpaulin used for covering barrows and the like. And neatly packaged with the final containing ties of industrial binding. His clothes tell us a little. Pocket debris and particles caught in the creases and folds.' Collins-Maynard stood; the chair gushed, escaping air with relief.

'Sodden, Leonard, we are on sodden ground where little stands up,' the chief superintendent concluded.

'One last narrow chance we can nail the killer,' Paul Leonard continued, 'is a partial DNA match.' Chief Superintendent Collins-Maynard was suddenly all ears. 'I obtained a DNA swab from that creep Bairstow yesterday.'

'A match?' interrupted Collins-Maynard, eager now, remaining standing.

'No.'

The superintendent reached once again for the rickety chair and slumped back down.

'It ruled Bairstow out. We had the partial unknown DNA

discovered in a fold in Demetrio's underwear. But it was a partial match for Craig Gayle. I understand it's not conclusive. There's little to go on. We do have this, though.' Paul Leonard studied his list. 'Definite motive, proximity to the Gayle home, market materials, relationship context, time convergence, DNA, silencing of a possible prosecution witness and, of course, we have a body this time.' Even a rookie policeman can recognise a case that has barely a concrete foundation, but Paul was building a strong base and was standing his ground well.

'So?' Collins-Maynard spoke through gritted teeth. 'You expect me to face the CPS with this list of piss-poor evidence? Again, I am going to be the laughing stock of the force. We have attempted to prosecute Craig Gayle once. It was a debacle. We cannot afford the same response or result. There's no case here, Detective Leonard, and I'm certain you know that. I can understand your frustration and even anger. File it. Maybe in the future, with some added testimony or evidence, we can place it on the table and proceed. For now it remains moribund. Bury it.'

'We have no one else. If we do not prosecute Craig Gayle, the case hits a wall. All our extensive work is wasted and a criminal goes free. Let me have the bastard here. Demetrio Natano would have been a crucial witness at Craig Gayle's murder trial and could have condemned him, rightfully. A fresh interview might bring us a result, might be able to squeeze the truth from him. We can't let him wriggle out of both cases. Two murders and he just laughs at us and continues, untouched, free. Free to murder again.' Paul Leonard wasn't actually spitting, probably pleading with the hint of a drizzle of saliva.

'I suppose it won't hurt,' the superintendent gasped. 'Keep me updated, and don't take this any further without confirmation from me. Email the questions you are going to ask him and your strategy to break down any fabrication he throws at you.'

With that, Collins-Maynard was off. The chair seemed to spring back with delight as he lifted himself from it, and he trudged towards the door. Paul Leonard piled up the documents, in a clerical manner, from his desk and tried to work out whether his meeting with the superintendent had been a success or not. When Warren Yates returned, he would arrange the interview with Craig Gayle. Little did he realise that Warren would return with further information that could herald a breakthrough in the Stephanie Gayle case as well. A conversation not quite as straightforward as he had assumed.

Chapter Twenty-One

'At the time of Gayle's missus disappearing like, I was working in Byfleet, at Golden Meadows, working the furnace,' Dean Wallace began telling Warren Yates across the table in the vast, now empty, visitor's hall. 'About four years ago or more.'

Outside the echoic space were the distant sounds of a prison mealtime, lines of inmates and herding officers. Almost Dickensian, institutionalised and drab. Occasional raised voices and the crash of crockery. In this visiting space, just two men remained; one strong-shouldered, straight-backed, alert and enquiring, the other hunched and miserable.

'Golden Meadows? Sounds like a nursing home,' responded Warren.

'It ain't no nursin' 'ome. It's a pet cemetery; that's what Golden Meadows is. It's where rich folk bury or burn their dogs and cats. Sometimes even a budgie.' Dean smirked a little; he didn't joke often or comfortably. 'Well, at the time, I'd 'ave a drink in the evening at the Fox and 'ounds at Weston Green. You need a drink after a day baking dead animals. There's people I sort of know in there.' Dean sucked in some air. He didn't know many people and found it hard to make friends. It wasn't something he was going to discuss with a policeman, or anybody. 'On this occasion, a guy comes up to talk to me. Just like that. Not someone I knew. Of course, I know 'im now. It was that Craig Gayle, who they tried for murdering 'is missus. Quite a shock when I seen 'im in the papers and on the box.'

'Craig Gayle spoke to you in this pub, the Fox and Hounds? What had he got to say?' Warren Yates was thrown awake by Dean's revelation.

'Started out all friendly, like. 'e wasn't a Craig then. Told me 'is name was Dave. Bought me a drink and began some talk about footer. I like that, don't know much, but when it comes to football I'm all ears and know the territory. 'e reckoned 'e's a local farmer and asks when I'm in the pub, 'ow it's been good chatting and that we should chat some more next time 'e's in. 'Ad my suspicions; didn't look like a farmer.' Dean looked around him, at the emptied prison visiting room and closely at Warren Yates. 'So, the next day I get to the pub, 'e's there. Wants to know what I do for a living. It seems, as I'm telling 'im, 'e already knows. Comes up with this cock and bull story about diseased animals on 'is farm and 'ow 'e 'as to get rid of 'em, their infected bodies, as a matter of urgency, government orders. In fact, 'e's late and the corpses should have been disposed of a week back.' Dean was on a roll now. 'Wasn't able to use the local animal facility and could 'e rent the incinerator at Golden Meadows so 'e could get this done? Wants to use it that evening. Agitated by the urgency. 'e offers me £500. Needed that. Couldn't turn 'im down. Had to show 'im the ropes, of course. Ain't simple that machinery.' Dean's eyes opened wide, and he seemed to search Warren's for forgiveness. 'Didn't know 'is real reason.'

Watching a play can often mean you drift off during the less intense or passionate parts. Your mind wanders, and you stick your brain into neutral. An explosion off stage, a sudden assassination and deathly scream; you're back there fully awakened. This production is hotting up. Warren Yates was thrown alert in the echoing prison visitors' hall. He was hearing stuff that was more than just relevant; it was hard evidence, right up his street. 'Let me get this clear. The guy in the pub, who you now recognise as Craig Gayle, claimed he was a farmer by the name of Dave. And this Dave asked to rent your furnace to incinerate dead livestock?'

'That's right,' Dean assured the policeman.

'About the same time Mrs Gayle disappeared?'

'You've got it,' Dean added, sliding back in his chair, a self-important glint in his eyes. The police inspector was hooked.

Warren Yates mulled over what he had just heard. 'And the next day, when you went back to the crematorium, what was there to see?'

'Well, there weren't any mess. 'e'd tidied up. Bit of crushin' necessary, of course. Pulverisin' is what we called it.' Dean seemed to be relishing this part. 'There's me believing 'e was torchin' a fucking 'erd of animals, but it seemed like 'e 'ad only burned a few, if that. 'e tells me that 'e 'as dumped the ashes. We 'ave this woodland area where people can sprinkle their animal's remains; they like that. So Dave tells me 'e's thrown a sprinkling there. I didn't check. The furnace was clean, well as clean as it usually is.'

*

Paul Leonard had to catch a tourist flight filled with bleating children and some unpleasant parents. From Lisbon, it was over two hours into the mountains by snorting bus. He was hot, uncomfortably hot. There are many black people in Portugal, but in the village of Vila Velha de Rodao, there were none. Paul Leonard stood out. Paul wasn't just black, he was British, and he was a detective. In a small settlement, he was news, and news was spread by doorstep whispers down the narrow cobbled roads between the red-tiled squat houses and among dusty-capped men over café coffees. All the inhabitants of this hillside village knew of Paul's arrival but were, as of now, unsure of its purpose. Communications with the regional authority merely confirmed the location of the Nantano family, at a place where he now stood. More of an oddity than a guest. No one approached the puzzling dark figure in the village square. They looked from windows, behind curtains and at doorways. It was up to Paul to break the ice. At a crumbling building that he identified as the police station, he pushed open the scrapping flaky blue door. In the middle of a cigarette smoke cloud, a middle-aged, moustachioed, rather overweight officer slouched at his desk. He looked up and surveyed Paul Leonard, his lips curled as if he would say something. He said nothing. More misty smoke. No words.

'The name's Detective Sergeant Paul Leonard. You should have been told of my arrival. The Metropolitan Police have been in touch.' Paul gulped; he sounded uneasy, and he was.

The Portuguese policeman puffed out more smoke and turned to papers on his desk. 'Sim,' he managed, waving a sheet aloft. Success at a desk weighed down by the burdens of red tape. He studied the content as if it wasn't something he hadn't read; it was. 'You are here to talk to the Nantano family, eh?' Coarse English, but Paul understood enough.

'Yes,' Paul responded, eager to flee the grubby office. 'It's part of an enquiry into a death in the UK.'

'You arrest somebody?' questioned the Portuguese policeman. 'No come here and it's that easy.'

'No arrests, no accusations, no crimes, no worries. I just

need to know some background about Demetrio Nantano, whose body was found in a reservoir. We believe he had been murdered.' Paul felt stupid saying that. There are no real reasons why a strangled corpse should be wrapped up and dumped in deep, concealing water and it not be a case of homicide.

The dusty policeman grunted and gestured approval with his head. 'I will bring someone. You wait here.' Paul shuffled outside; he wasn't spending any more time in that fume-filled place.

It was about half an hour before the sloppy policeman returned. Accompanying him was a stocky, swarthy individual, squat and square, local moustache, spiky stubble and sweeping black hair. A man of the fields and open air. Weather-beaten. Not unhandsome in a rough way. From an opposing direction came another, elderly, gentleman. Tidier yet rather worn at the edges, frayed cuffs, well-worn suit, high swinging trousers around his ankles belted at the stomach, waistline at his chest, with more of a smile than the other two men.

Pushing the younger man forward with a heavy shove. 'This here is Demetrio's brother. He speaks no English. I bring also the village interpreter.' The policeman indicated the older man, who lifted his grubby hat and gave what seemed a bow. 'You can use a room at the police headquarters,' the officer continued.

Headquarters, Paul thought, were they off to a fine and fitting establishment? No, the policeman indicated a small, dark room next to his foggy office.

'Fine.' Paul tried to sound appreciative.

The three men sat at a small rickety table. 'My name is Alfonso Borsata, and I am here to assist,' the old man began.

'This young man is Mateo Nantano, the brother of Demetrio. It is my job, which I hope I do well, is to translate your questions and his answers. Do you wish to ask me anything?'

Paul Leonard thanked him. There were no questions to ask the interpreter. Each man scuffled a chair forward. Only their breathing could be heard; Alfonso's louder than the others. 'You understand that your brother's body was found in a reservoir in the UK? He had been murdered. I am here to confirm the bad news and to see if you can shine any light on, sorry, find out what happened and who did this.' Paul was aware that he needed to be clear and his language easy to translate.

Alfonso spluttered all this out in Portuguese. Mateo nodded. He lit a cigarette. An especially smelly one that you get on the continent. More donkey dung than tobacco.

'We believe his death is related to another case we are dealing with. A woman who went missing a while ago. It's possible she was murdered by her husband, Craig Gayle. We know that your brother knew this man.' Paul tried to hide a knowing glimpse. 'At Gayle's trial, we expected to use Demetrio as a witness, but he had disappeared. Naturally thought he'd fled back to Portugal to escape the publicity. Could be Demetrio was killed by Gayle to keep him quiet. When did you last see or talk to Demetrio?' Paul questioned. Mateo shrugged his shoulders, puffed a large cloud of smoke, twisted his mouth and responded to Alfonso. Unlike the interpreter, Mateo's voice was coarse and guttural. A deep and throaty response that lasted for some time.

'He says it was at least two years ago,' Alfonso announced. 'It wasn't a happy time; apparently they didn't get on. Demetrio was, how you say, the black sheep of the family. When they heard of your arrival in the village, his parents and other family members were reluctant to speak to you. They are ashamed of Demetrio. Mateo says that's why he left Vila Velha de Rodao and hid himself in Britain.'

Mateo started breathing heavily as if trying to control some inner anger. He raised himself from his chair, creased face, eyes blazing. 'Paneleiro!' Mateo spread his arms across the table, gritted his teeth and repeated, 'Paneleiro!' Seething and spitting, his eyes even wider and hateful. He pulled back, head swinging.

'Paneleiro? What is that?' Paul Leonard was taken aback, shocked by Mateo's sudden movement and outcry.

Alfonso held a resigned smile on his face. 'Gay. Demetrio was, as you say, gay. Not one member of the family could embrace that. He was the outcast. There was no place for a homosexual in their family or village. In this rural area of Portugal, they accept only what they think is normal behaviour and the usual sexual orientation. Man chases and then marries woman, there are children. It's that simple. Such alternative relationships and fancies are consigned to the cities, or other countries.

Mateo was aware that the British detective had grasped the reason for his anger and disappointment and began mumbling more. Alfonso did his best to keep up with another outburst and would turn to Mateo for clarification. More cigarettes. A clouded room.

'When you spoke to your brother on his last visit, what did he say? Did he mention the man he had been seeing?' Paul questioned further.

Alfonso turned to the now slumped Mateo. He spoke slower and with gentle tones. He knew Demetrio's brother's head was wading through the soreness of his brother's last visit.

Mateo gulped and responded sluggishly. 'There had been arguments and much pain,' Alfonso explained. 'But he says that his brother was frightened by the man, Gayle, and feared his anger. A scared Demetrio told him that Gayle had killed his wife; that worried him a great deal that this man was a murderer.'

Paul Leonard almost jumped from his chair. 'Mateo tells you that his brother was told by Craig Gayle that he had slaughtered his wife, Stephanie? It's what we have been looking for, a witness. I know Demetrio can't give evidence, but his brother can. We are able to, at last, pin him down. It doesn't seem unreasonable that Gayle also murdered Demetrio to avoid detection.' Paul was almost excited.

Alfonso pulled at Mateo's arm and spoke soothingly. A glum response. 'Mateo is of a similar opinion about the fate of his brother,' he assured Paul Leonard.

'Finally,' Paul began, 'Mateo, did Demetrio tell you what Gayle did with his wife's, Stephanie's, body?'

Mateo straightened up and threw his waving arms in the air. His breath sizzled and sparked. 'Demetrio's male friend had confided in his paramour, begrudgingly, that,' Alfonso faltered, 'that he had burned her, taken her somewhere and devastated her remains by fire, destroyed that poor woman.'

*

'Torched 'er. That shit had fried 'er.' Dean fell quiet, an incendiary thought winging through his head.

In a while, now composed. 'Not much 'ad been going on. It weren't until Gayle's trial and 'is photo in the paper that it dawned on me the possibility that 'e 'ad cooked 'is missus. Put 'er into the flames. Got rid of the body that way. Felt really bad, as if I was part of the plan, involved. Of course, I weren't.' Dean looked into Warren's eyes to declare his innocence. 'Not like I 'ad the money to give back to 'im. Long gone. Didn't stay at Golden Meadows for long after that. Now can't stop thinking about the poor woman's body blazing away in me oven.' Dean relaxed back in his chair. There, he'd done it. Off his chest. Things like this can haunt you, keep a man awake at night.

'So, Dean, you are claiming that Craig Gayle wanted to use your incinerator at the pet cemetery in order to get rid of his wife's body? So that no trace would be found?' Warren Yates was beyond puzzled. Where could he start to find evidence of this event? Was it possible to support it? Was this man telling the truth? 'How could I prove this actually took place? What should I be looking for?'

'Since 'e used the crematorium, there 'ave been 'undreds of roasted animal bodies that 'ave gone through that furnace. Won't find anything. No knowing where 'e dumped the ashes, been too long anyway. It's me word. You've got to believe me.' Dean was empty. He'd done his job, told the police how it was.

Warren Yates stood. Tall and straight. Something left over from the military or police academy at Hendon. Pulled his coat off the back of his chair, ready to go. 'Just one more thing,' Warren started. 'How come you were able to contact Kirsty Foster? Don't take this the wrong way, but you do not seem a technologically skilled person, a computer wizard.' Warren attempted to make it not seem demeaning.

'In the clink, places like this, there's a right mixture. We aren't all thieves and killers. Well, locked up with me, sharing a cell, was this guy who used 'is computer to trick people into giving 'im money; fucking scammer. Got away with it for several months, but you coppers are learning quickly and 'e was caught. So many quiet hours in 'ere. We got talking. I mentioned about Gayle and the crematorium, and 'e 'elped me, see. Now 'e was an Internet wizard 'e was.'

Warren was eager to get back to the office. Fresh evidence brings fresh enthusiasm. A quick glance back at Dean as he shuffled towards a prison officer, heading for the delights of his cell. 'You are willing to tell the court exactly what you've told me, aren't you?' Warren urged in a raised voice.

'Not sure,' came the strangled reply. Dean caught sight of the portly frame of Buggy, his dark eyes focused, watching Dean's every move from just inside the corridor. To agree to a police officer's request in his earshot, Dean knew, would be unwise. What time he had left at Pentonville, he wanted to survive intact.

Chapter Twenty-Two

Paul Leonard thought he had broken the case and held the secret that had evaded them. Stephanie Gayle had been grotesquely disposed of by fire. Although he was extremely tired, returning from Portugal, he couldn't wait to break the news to his superior. Nothing like holding the trump card. Unfortunately, he was unaware that Warren too was a bearer of the same news; a similar excitement. Snap. Stephanie Gayle's incineration was his surprise for his sergeant, or so he thought.

The two men arrived at their cramped office within minutes of each other. Both with broad, smiling, satisfied faces, bursting to tell of their discovery.

Paul Leonard exploded first. 'Result. A trip worth taking. Listen to this, Demetrio Nantano told his brother that Stephanie's body had been burned following her death at the hands of Craig Gayle. The bastard had her incinerated.'

'He's right,' a slightly outmanoeuvred Warren Yates declared. 'Found out the same thing over here. The charming inmate, Dean Wallace, explained in detail how Craig Gayle rented a furnace at the local pet cemetery, where Dean worked, to destroy her body and any evidence of the cause of death. A long and, at times, tedious interview with the villain tidied this case up for me.' Warren Yates was flat. All the enthusiasm that he took to the office was extinguished. His sergeant had played the trump card.

In an effort to reinvigorate him, Paul Leonard, still chirpy, suggested the next move. He had already agreed with Chief Superintendent Collins-Maynard that bringing Gayle in for questioning over the discovery of Demetrio Nantano's body was justified; now, with this crucial evidence, they had slack to play with. 'Surely we can close in on this guy. He's the most likely person to have silenced Demetrio Nantano. We have a smidgen of DNA that helps, two witnesses to the manner of disposal of Stephanie Gayle's body and...' Paul was sure there was something else but couldn't recall it. 'Yes, and there's the market paraphernalia that Nantano was wrapped in; definitely New Covent Garden attire. All this, along with motive, opportunity and, hopefully, evidence.'

'Get all we have documented, plan out the interview, and we'll bring Gayle in. He's a crafty bloke and knows the ropes. We mustn't fuck this up, Paul.' Detective Inspector Warren Yates had the nagging feeling that this case was still wobbly and didn't have the legs it needed. 'One piece of concrete proof, please.' Warren looked skyward as if pleading to the heavens.

*

Craig Gayle was toying with his cars when the call came. The police as polite as they could be. He cursed that, yet again, he was being hauled in for questioning. However, this time there wasn't the dawn raid and the swarms of Old Bill pulling his house apart and digging up his garden. No visit at all. More or less a kindly invite to call in for a chat. An inconvenience but unlikely to be anything serious.

By chance, Kirsty was loading the kids into the car when Gayle cruised past on his way to the police station. She wouldn't look. Craig Gayle managed the usual sneer. Justine saw him but said nothing. She knew how her mother's anxiety was easily fuelled. Charlie clicked in his seatbelt, and Elliot kept his eyes on the pages of his revision book. Tom was long gone on his commute to work. There were a few people who knew now what had happened to Stephanie, but Kirsty was still oblivious. She hadn't yet learned that her very best, beautiful friend had met such a sordid fate. The unceremonious flames that had destroyed her once so alluring, but now stone dead, body. Shovelled out of a furnace and scattered who knows where. Kirsty's crusade was at an abrupt halt. Unaware of the vile act, she drove onward, ready to distribute her kids at their respective schools. Of course, she would sit in front of her computer and search Stephanie's 'scribble wall'. Not much action now. Was the interest, the mutual appeal waning, disappearing like Stephanie herself? At the moment, Kirsty was being kept in the dark. Warren Yates would tell her soon. Not a task he relished.

*

Wimbledon police station was old, not Robert Peel old, but barely post-war. The interview room where Craig Gayle was to be questioned, where he had been before, boasted only a rectangular table and some stackable chairs. On the table, sat at one end, was a mangle of wires that spilled from a recording apparatus.

Craig Gayle was led there by the brusque desk sergeant; given time to settle, look around and contemplate. It was procedure. Yates bustled in about ten minutes later, carrying folders. Paul Leonard waited, yet to play his part. No one was going to be pleasant. Too many memories.

'Mr Gayle, you are here merely to discuss aspects of our case, not cautioned or arrested,' Paul Leonard informed him. Craig Gayle tilted his head up and down in acknowledgement. 'You do not need a legal companion.'

Warren Yates spread his folder open, papers pulled and fanned out. 'The body of your friend Demetrio Nantano has been found in Island Barn Reservoir. Bound and sunken, weighted and hidden until he floated to the surface. He is a man that you knew intimately, I believe?'

'Yes.' Gayle announced. Quite unlike the 'no comment' replies of the previous questioning. Warren Yates feared that this response was more problematic.

'If you recall, this man disappeared just before your trial for the murder of your wife?' Warren continued. 'It was thought he had returned to his native Portugal. A wrong assumption. No, he had been brutally murdered. You not only knew Demetrio, but you were also involved in a homosexual relationship with him, weren't you?'

'Yes,' Gayle agreed timidly, 'I knew this guy, and we were together for a while.'

'Nantano's disappearance suited you, didn't it? There was probably quite a lot he could tell us. Well, poor old Demetrio suffered severe injuries before being packaged up in market trappings and consigned to the deep water of the local reservoir. Did you kill Demetrio Nantano?' Warren Yates pressed his face closer. 'Was this your way of silencing this young man?' The inspector could not help slipping into interrogation mode.

'No,' replied Craig Gayle, a man of few words. He crossed and uncrossed his legs and stared out of the misty window.

'Of course, we understand the nature of your relationship with Demetrio.' Warren smiled knowingly. 'A relationship where you could easily talk and possibly say too much, eh? A person couldn't be certain that once confided with an awful secret, that individual doesn't tell close friends or family. Have you ever considered this, Craig?' Warren's knowing, glowing face pressed closer to Gayle's. 'Don't you think he told someone? Killing Nantano was a waste of time, wasn't it? The terrible confidence that you whispered to your young boyfriend at the pillow was thumping inside your head. You couldn't let him say anything to a jury. But little did you know that he had spilled the beans to members of his family. The secret did not die with poor Demetrio as you intended.'

Gayle became uneasy. Not an agitation that he would show the policeman. All he could manage was a despairing sigh and eyes back to the window. Breathing heavier.

Paul Leonard entered the interview room. He had waited for this pause and carried a police evidence plastic bag. Paul proceeded to pull a collection of evidence bags, with some hopefully incriminating contents, out onto the table. Gayle was faced with a scratchy worn blue canvas tarpaulin and shredded twine. A collection he was familiar with.

'Recognise these?' enquired Warren Yates.

'Yeah.' Now he demonstrated his unease with a heavy snort through his nose and what sounded like a gulp. 'You know they're from the market, where I work, where hundreds work. You're barking up the wrong tree, Inspector.' Gayle wouldn't look at the stuff for long.

'Demetrio Nantano's funeral garb. It's what we found him bound in. Whoever killed this young man tied him up in all this and dumped him, weighted, into the water. It was you, wasn't it?' Warren shuffled his chair closer to Gayle. 'These items were around you every day, and when you choked the life out of this guy, you parcelled him up in all this.' Warren waved his hand over the items on the table. 'Just down the road, Island Barn Reservoir, so simple to unload him there; convenient, eh?'

Gayle didn't speak. As if events were twirling round his head. 'You've got some imagination, you have,' Gayle eventually garbled. 'I've told you, it weren't me.'

The two policemen would let him dwell. Let him look at the rope and the tarpaulin. Let him resolve any torment or guilt. A quiet room. Contemplation time. It was part of the investigation process. They would launch the second assault next.

Warren closed in. 'You found somewhere or someone in order to complete your sordid task. Didn't you?' Warren was expelling biting words along with a scything breath.

'Where are you going?' Gayle chirped. 'Nothing to find out here.' Craig Gayle pulled himself straight-backed and exhaled audibly through his nose. 'I hope you aren't going to be long; I'm getting tired.' His legs quivered, and he tried to stifle a swallow.

'Incineration. Cremation on the cheap.' Warren Yates was as close to Gayle's face as he dared. 'We know how your poor wife was made to disappear. You killed her and chose this gruesome method to dispose of this lovely woman.' Craig Gayle shrank back, almost rocking his chair. Face clammy, shoulders twitching. 'Some time after your wife's killing, you took her corpse to some location and burned her body as if incinerating waste.'

'Well, of course, to you she was waste, waste that had to be removed, telling evidence of your vile deed,' Paul Leonard added. 'And in the cosiness of the bed, you needed to admit such to that poor wretch Demetrio Nantano. Perhaps to demonstrate that this woman fed to the flames was an incineration of that side of your sexual appetite, eh?'

Craig Gayle resembled a man who had lost his 'get out of jail free' card. A mouth ajar without a sound, as a goldfish gulping air. He pitched back and forth. No eyes for the policemen. 'No, no,' he finally muttered. 'Didn't kill my wife, didn't burn her. Been in court for all this shit before. As you know, I'm an innocent man.' A dilute voice, stumbling over his words.

'So, Craig, we are wrong? No, you used a furnace to destroy any remains of Stephanie. And your motive was that no one was going to find her whole, identifiable. Just anonymous ash; disappearance without trace.' Warren leaned back in his chair, a smirk of triumph on his face. 'You did it all right.'

Craig Gayle was not going to be trapped. He was used to dancing around the law, and this inspector wasn't in a position to nail this wriggler. He breathed in and out several times. Breathing that Warren Yates could hear. Gayle's eyes opened extra wide; he half raised himself, hands gripping the table. He glared into the police officer's eyes. 'It ain't me. No, you ain't going to stick this one on me. We've had all this crap before. They found me innocent, not guilty, set up.' Now a mixture of arrogance and annoyance in his voice. 'You can't try and pin this on me again. No, only the once. Know the law.'

Craig Gayle was off. Warren Yates stood alongside him, livid. He felt the urge to punch Gayle, and maybe kick him a bit. Horrible little shit. Warren spoke on the move, following Gayle away from the table. 'We know what happened to Stephanie. You killed your wife, and you fucking shoved her lifeless body in a furnace and reduced her to ashes. We will prove it.'

Gayle skulked out of the door like a retreating hyena.

Dean Wallace would never have considered himself a secret weapon, would barely have understood. Warren Yates watched Gayle leave the station knowing, but yet to realise its use, that he was concealing a card up his sleeve. Not a very reliable one, but it was all he had. Dean Wallace might yet be of use.

Chapter Twenty-Three

Chief Superintendent Collins-Maynard pushed piles of papers around his desk. Wimbledon was awash with burglaries, and each crime created a mountain of paperwork. Paperwork that he wouldn't read, but relocating the stacks somehow helped. Warren Yates was about to phone him. The sudden ringing churned the stomach of Collins-Maynard. It always meant a problem. It rang even louder, it seemed, that morning.

'Yes,' came the limp reply. 'Oh, Inspector Yates, good morning.' He was right; here came another problem, well, an old one that repeatedly raised its ugly head.

'It's the Stephanie Gayle case, sir,' Warren Yates started. 'New evidence has been unearthed. We briefly interviewed the husband, Craig Gayle, over the discovery of Demetrio Nantano's body, but events have accelerated our knowledge in this case. My assistant, Paul Leonard, has been to Portugal to talk to Demetrio's family, and I have uncovered an unpleasant scenario from a Mr Dean Wallace. Both lines of enquiry have resulted in the breakthrough. It appears that Stephanie Gayle was piled into a furnace and burned beyond all recognition by her husband.'

'Cremated?' Collins-Maynard snapped.

'Yes, sir. Wallace confirms that Craig Gayle hired the furnace facility at Golden Meadows pet cemetery for this purpose, and Mateo Nantano, Demetrio's brother, has informed us that Demetrio told him about Gayle's crime during

Nantano's visit home. This bastard not only killed his wife, he incinerated her as well.'

'Shit.' Collins-Maynard wasn't sure that he uttered such a curse out of horror or the thought of an impending enquiry that wouldn't go away. 'Is this enough to drag him through the courts again? The CPS is going to have to look long and hard at this case. Those civil servants don't like resurrecting moribund judgements, especially double jeopardy cases. It's a maze out there when someone's been acquitted previously.'

'I'll give them all I have, and hopefully an eager lawyer in the department will get off his arse and chase Gayle down. Now I had better let Kirsty Foster know what we've discovered. She has been the catalyst and the driver in this case. Only right.' Warren wasn't feeling buoyed by the prospect. Who would choose to explain to someone that their gorgeous best friend has been burned to a cinder?

Tom answered the door when Warren Yates and Paul Leonard arrived. Kids were still up, playing games, finishing homework or being instructed how to do so by an ever-insistent Kirsty. The two detectives were sat in the lounge as children were shepherded to their rooms. Their squeaky voices could be heard high in the distance. Tom accompanied his wife to hear what the police had to say. He hoped their visit signalled the end of this trouble, that Kirsty could let go of her desperate quest.

Formalities over and pleasantries exchanged, Warren began. 'Since we last spoke, Kirsty, there have been new revelations in the case of your missing friend, Stephanie Gayle.'

A smile spread across Kirsty's face.

'Sounds encouraging,' Tom chipped in, arms around his wife's shoulders. Little did the Fosters realise that all news is not good news.

'Your dearest friend, Stephanie,' began Warren, 'most likely came to an ignominious end. Brave yourself, Kirsty. From Sergeant Leonard's enquiries in Portugal and my meeting with this character you led us to, Dean, we have to accept that Stephanie Gayle's body will never be found and that her killer will most probably never be brought to justice; though we are trying. Stephanie was, if our investigation is correct, cremated by her husband, Craig Gayle.'

In an explosion of tears and flying spittle, Kirsty sprang from her seat. 'Cremated? How do you mean?'

'Well, it wasn't a cremation that we all understand, at a crematorium with family and friends of the deceased. Furtively done. Gayle, the malevolent bastard, rented the furnace in a pet cemetery, Golden Meadows, and disposed of her body. Dean Wallace, who worked there, has confirmed Gayle's use of that facility and Mateo Nantano, Demetrio's brother, informs us that Demetrio told him, back in Portugal, that Gayle had confessed to burning his wife's body.' Warren Yates paused, waiting for the near wailing to subside.

'Steph burned to death. I just can't imagine her terror. Her beautiful body just ashes.' Kirsty collapsed back into Tom's arms. Her brain was trying to reject some awful images of Stephanie's body being consumed by searing fire, the soft facial skin peeling with a sizzle, her flowing hair rapidly singeing. She could almost smell it.

'Most probably dead before she was put in the fire,' Paul Leonard added. Paul was a man who liked to ensure everything was correct. Kirsty didn't hear him. Nothing was happening outside her head.

'You mean to say this monster murdered his wife, and

before he reported her missing he set her alight to destroy all evidence of his crime? All this time searching for Stephanie. You can see this has been wrecking my wife.' Tom had stood and was, for once, vocal. 'Justice? What about arresting him again and putting him on trial? You can't just watch him get away with this. We can't bear him walk or motor past us, knowing what he has done. It's grotesque.'

'We will, of course, be consulting with the Crown Prosecution Service. Gayle's first trial was a mistake. If we'd had this new evidence, we probably could have succeeded in court. Now there's only a slim possibility the CPS will chance another hearing. Especially with the many financial cutbacks. Not worth the gamble if he's bound to worm his way out of this.' Warren Yates could offer little hope. No one was listening. He was the infamous messenger, and he knew it.

Warren and Paul slid away quietly with just a nod to Tom. *Thanks,* he thought as he bundled up his sobbing wife. It would be a dreadful night.

Chapter Twenty-Four

Kirsty Foster didn't sleep that night, as expected. She let Tom have a fractured slumber, waking every half hour to check on her. Tumbling through her head came the repeated violence of Stephanie's death and a final despicable dumping. Where was she now? Well, what Craig Gayle had left of her? No grave to visit. No garden of remembrance. Nowhere Kirsty could take flowers, say her goodbyes, keep tidy. Some dignity. No, just ditched ashes. Not even a funeral pot for the mantelpiece; thrown, spread, tramped on, hidden. Stephanie, oh Stephanie.

And when, at first light, she drifted into a tormented sleep, Kirsty had some swirling dreams. Amidst the bright and sun-filled perfection of their friendship came a conjured-up vision of Maureen Atkins. She was garbling on about Little Miss Bump. With a start, Kirsty was awake again.

'You okay?' Tom quizzed, alarmed by Kirsty's sudden movement.

'Little Miss Bump, Little Miss Bump.'

Tom was unsure about his wife's state of mind. 'Settle down. Try and sleep a little. You need the rest.'

'Steph was called Little Miss Bump because she smashed her body on a school trip. She had to have metal rods inserted to fix the breaks. They were never removed. If that shit cremated Steph, then surely the rods survived and can be identified, found. Find the metal rods, and you find Steph's ashes.' Kirsty breathed deeply. 'We haven't been able to save her, but we can discover a final resting place.'

Tom was less enthusiastic. There aren't heaps of ashes decorated with lengths of surgical steel lying around these crematoriums. 'Don't get too carried away. I'm sure these places have to deal with all sorts of things that don't burn. Even with animals. We are talking about a long time ago.' Tom could see Kirsty was grasping any thread. 'Look, I'll make some enquiries later today. Find out how it works, what happens to the stuff that isn't flammable. Okay?' Tom was desperate to calm his anxious wife.

Kirsty slept. She slept until mid-afternoon. When she did prise herself from bed, her eye sockets were black and sunken, her hair wild, her mouth dry. She didn't care. Tom was out, and the children had been warned to tread carefully, gently with their mother. They stayed in their rooms until they heard Kirsty up and about.

She was in the kitchen when Tom returned. Bad news written in his glum look. He grabbed Kirsty and held her tightly at the shoulders. As reassuringly as he could. His voice a whisper. 'No luck, dear. They sell them. All the metal they collect at these crematoria is recycled. Waste is money. Apparently, they need to detect the pacemakers early on as they explode in that heat. Didn't know dogs were fitted. And the surgical steel that has been used to mend broken limbs is extracted using a large electromagnet from the pile of ashes. Tons of the stuff they find each month. Nothing remains. Nothing is kept. You get your pot of ash. Usually.'

Kirsty sighed and sat at the kitchen island, head in hands. There was no pot for Stephanie. She wasn't coming back in body, soul or plastic container.

'Sorry I couldn't bring better news, dear.' Tom stayed to

comfort his wife.

The next night was yet again a torment. Kirsty's mind was whirling. Steph's horribly torched body was there, the clanking of metal parts dragged along by a huge magnet and being separated from a pile of ashes, buzzing of fidgeting pacemakers, more flames. A night's torture showed on her face. Mentally bruised. Kirsty's children were used to their mother being below par in the morning. They spoke little and shuffled around the kitchen, preparing themselves for school. Tom would drive them.

When he returned, Kirsty was still not dressed, iPad on her knees, bent forward on the sofa. It doesn't take long to provide a desperate woman with a fresh crusade. She was reliving comments on the wall. Particularly those of Maureen Atkins. In reaction to Maureen's tales of Little Miss Bump, she tapped in an enquiry about which resort in France Stephanie had had her accident, and when it was. Maureen was slow coming back. Mainly because she was vague after all this time and had phoned others from that trip to confirm. It was two days before a reply came scratching on the wall. Resort named but dates vague. Kirsty could work with this.

What she had in mind came whirring out of the blue. As if her battery had been recharged. Tom was stunned.

At dinner that evening, Kirsty tested the water. 'Who fancies a skiing holiday at half-term?' she declared. A family startled by Kirsty's new-found energy and sudden passion.

'What?' Justine stammered. 'You don't like skiing. I'm not too keen myself.'

'This is news,' her husband queried. 'Skiing? Sounds like a great idea. Can't say I'm not surprised by your enthusiasm.'

Elliot came alive, was glowing. 'Wow, just up my street.

That would be great.'

Charlie was unsure, but he knew he did like snow.

The diners were animated for a long while. No one could understand Kirsty's sudden keenness for what she used to consider a cold and unpleasant sport. However, they were grateful she was focused elsewhere, a refreshing new pursuit.

'I'll need the right gear,' announced Justine, imagining her appearance on the slopes. She scuttled off to search the Internet for the latest skiwear.

'Risoul, French Alps,' Kirsty proclaimed. 'That's where we'll go.'

Tom was still reeling. 'You've got this all worked out, dear.'

'I have,' she responded. But what Kirsty had got worked out was quite different from the buzz of the skiers. There were plans afoot that this excited little family was unaware of. The campaign box belonging to the search for Stephanie had not been sealed for long, and was springing open yet again.

Half-term was several weeks away, but the Foster family plans began and would continue until departure. Cases were packed, every eventuality and every climatic condition prepared for. The children had all their skiwear, and Tom had bought a fine Nevica suit that he paraded around the house in on many occasions. Franz Klammer?

Ryanair from Stansted isn't classy travelling. The Foster children never noticed. Kids don't. Turin airport was better. It was going to be a long transfer to Risoul. Tom fell asleep soon after the bus left the airport, and the children were napping shortly after. Kirsty's mind was purring with a devious plan. She didn't nod off.

Risoul isn't one of the most attractive resorts in the French Alps. Not one that the glitterati frequent or the most skilful skiers seek out. School groups, novice snowboarders, clumsy middle-agers who could hack down some gentle green slopes and complete beginners, in the most. None of the hotels could boast five stars, or if they did, they were lying. Comfortable family guesthouses with welcoming locals, where the mother ran the lodge, the father managed the lift system, and the kids worked as ski instructors or served in the local bars. A family affair. It was one such hostel that Kirsty had booked online. Most of the photos had been taken years ago, and the interior was now tired. They were going to be on the mountain skiing all day, so it didn't matter that much. Kirsty herself worried least.

Everyone slept well. More exhaustion from the journey than the comfort of the beds. It was an early start; ski hire, lift passes, piste map studying. Ski school for Charlie.

'Come on, Mum, you'll enjoy it,' encouraged Elliot. 'What are you going to do all day?' He couldn't persuade his mother. Kirsty was happy to ensure everyone was warm and the equipment was comfortable. She had no intention of using this trip to slide down those slopes.

'Follow me.' Franz Klammer beckoned his kids towards the line forming at the bottom of the cable car. 'I'll show you how to prevent queue jumpers and which pistes you should tackle.'

Kirsty retreated to a small café at the foot of the run into the village. She could observe the lower slopes from there. She could plan from there. A small Americano lasted an hour. Some resort workers came in and slumped at a table. Kirsty summoned up the courage. Quite the actress.

'Sorry to trouble you, but my friend has been injured on the mountain. A fracture of the leg. I am not certain to which hospital they have taken her. Could you help?'

Several sun-crisped, wrinkled heads glumly turned, shoulders shrugging, obviously no grasp of the English language. A younger man at a neighbouring stall shot to his feet. Ready to display his knowledge of the English language.

'Can I help?' he asked, smiling broadly.

'The local hospital. Where skiers are taken to?' Kirsty continued. 'Is it the same with every injury?'

'Hospital Centre Des Escartons. It's the only one. Unless you really smash your head in, then they'll carry you further to Grenoble or Lyon. It's got to be bad, life-threatening, to take you that far, and I'm talking about several hours of some precarious motoring.'

'Hospital Centre Des Escartons,' Kirsty repeated; not quite with the same eloquence as her young helper, an instructor by the wording on his ski suit. 'Thank you.' The youthful ski teacher sat back down to his coffee, pleased he could help the tourist.

It would be the next day before Kirsty made a further move. There was all the frantic departure of the skiers, gloves, passes, goggles. Charlie taken by Tom to the ski kiddies group, and the older kids joining the long line of enthusiasts at the chair lift. Kirsty fetching hats, securing boots, checking bindings and finding lost snoods. It was a glorious day, the sun in a vivid blue sky and barely a wind. Just the day to… catch a bus. Kirsty scrabbled aboard the slush-splashed, grey coach that would take her to Briançon. The city that housed the hospital; the highest city in France, so her web page told her. After a snaking journey up torturous terrain, Kirsty climbed from the bus and trudged towards the hospital, which she knew was on the edge of Briançon, lofty, concrete, perched on the mountain side.

All hospitals smell the same. A lingering commotion. Was it buzz or chaos? People rushing in scattered directions. White coats flapping. Quick conversations. Earnest discussion. Trolleys, patients and the seated. Many seated. Rows of anxious faces, some stuck in the tatty magazines freely available. Kirsty didn't know where to go or who to ask. A reception counter looked promising, although the receptionist far from approachable. Middle-aged and middle class, sour and grim.

Kirsty waited until there was a gap in the straggling queue and stood at the counter. The miserable woman eyed her up and down with a face that was far from welcoming. Kirsty's French was sparse and probably incomprehensible. As with most English people, she hoped and probably expected any foreigner to speak her language. With luck it was just a 'what do you want' glance.

'Do you speak English?' Kirsty enquired.

There was a pause and an even more disgruntled face. 'I can do,' came the surly reply. An obvious reluctance.

'It's about a patient who was treated here nearly thirty years ago.' Kirsty was aware how weird her request was. 'I know it's a long way back, but it is very important to me now.' Kirsty was almost pleading with the caustic face peering over the counter at her.

'Les archives,' came the curt reply. 'Jose will help.' The disagreeable woman pored over a pile of papers at the same time as hailing Jose on the phone. Kirsty retreated to a seat. Before long, a shambling, bespectacled man puffed his way up some neighbouring stairs. He stopped and surveyed the waiting area after pulling off his glasses. Who had called him from his beautiful dungeon of papers, files and assorted cardboard boxes? Like a nocturne pulled awake; the light forcing him to screw up his wrinkled eyes. A sour voice groaned from the reception desk. 'Madame,' she managed, pointing an accusing finger in Kirsty's direction.

'My French is not good,' Kirsty mumbled.

'Do not have worries; I enjoy using my English,' Jose added, something like a grin on his pale face. He seldom spoke to anyone all day; it was the nature of the job. Most of the time that's how he liked it. 'How am I able to help?'

'Do you keep medical records here in the hospital? I mean, not recent ones. Perhaps thirty years. Not sure of the exact date.' Kirsty garbled, knew it was all vague. 'I have names.'

Jose held his nose and sucked in some hospital air. In pursuit of another needle in the haystack. 'Let's go down to my place, my den, where I am keeping these records. Not certain I'm allowed to be a broadcaster of, how you say, sensitive information. We'll see.' He was well aware of the rules, well aware of when he could break them, and well aware he liked to show he was his own boss.

Jose's archive was a shadowy cellar crammed with files and towering cabinets and shelves. A not-unpleasant odour of old cardboard. He strode through aisles as if it was his palace; the owner. It was. 'Now let's see if we are tracking this down,' Jose smirked and looked up through his glasses that perched at the tip of his nose. In front of him, on a high desk, were books; bound and heaped. Jose chose an approximate tome. None of this stored on a disk or merely plug-in a memory stick; nothing so simple, nothing so convenient.

There was something Dickensian about Jose, his walnut desk and his growls as he thumbed through his records. 'If I had the exact date, it would be only the little problem,' he muttered, 'as it is, what with the many skis accidents we get every year, this is going to be difficult.'

'Probably about twenty-eight to thirty years ago, I'm afraid,' Kirsty squeaked. 'Her name was Stephanie Pollard then. Yes, that would be the name you're looking for.' Kirsty pulled away from the little man's endeavours, embarrassed by the task she had set him.

Jose began. Briskly he bustled down the precarious towering aisles. A new energy. Jose liked a challenge; examining some browning files with the odour of history. Doctors long gone; only learned scribble in faded blue ink. A physician's cherished fountain pen. Jose's finger jabbed and followed rows of names and dates. A knowing finger guided by an eagle eye. There were lists of foreign names mingled with home-grown monikers. He searched as Kirsty sat watching the beavering actions of the archivist. He was a terrier at the foxhole, digging and filtering. Sighs and puffs but no words. Occasionally stopping at some interesting treatments and comments. Something like a smile breaking Jose's intense expression.

'Ah, yes,' Jose spluttered. 'Fourteenth February 1987 treated by Monsieur Clemence, orthopaedic surgeon, remember him well. I think this is what you are looking for.' Jose held the file flat to his chest as if clutching treasure. 'Now, am I going to let you look at this?' He sat down. Kirsty shuffled closer. Jose spread the papers out, fanning them across his desk. He wasn't going to hold back. 'Bruising, much bruising,' Jose muttered. He turned the page. Surgery. 'Your Stephanie Pollard was in theatre. A fractured femur and finger. Badly broken. Supporting metallic insertions. Steel rod in her leg and a very small tantalum plate holding the finger together. She was a mess, no?' Jose listed injuries and remedy. Pleased with himself. 'And madame, each of these splints that keep our bodies together is of fine craftsmanship and catalogue etched with a number of the identification. You see here,' Jose poked a twisted finger to a separate column, 'is it not shown that the steel rod was AC231783 and the little finger repair completed with tantalum shard T466613? Difficult to read with the naked eye. Remarkable, no?'

'Can I get a copy of those documents?' Kirsty pleaded.

Jose blew out some air, audibly. 'Let us be seeing if this is possible.' He scooped up the papers and headed to a small alcove at the back of the cellar. Kirsty was going to get her copies. Jose fed the frail paper through the chugging photocopier. The originals browning with age. Kirsty's sheets gleaming white.

'Thank you.' Kirsty was extremely pleased and grateful to the archivist. She left with a smile for the kindly man, who shuffled back down to his cave. A gerbil returning to his hole.

With documents housed safely in her handbag, Kirsty headed back to Risoul. A beam of satisfaction fixed on her face. Even the slush and the icy wind was pure background. Mission complete. Not that she was sure this new information could help. She was soon to find out that it most definitely would.

'How was your day?' Tom asked when the straggling skiers tramped down from the mountain. Flushed with success yet noticeably worn and weary.

'Great, I had a great day.' Kirsty's radiant face greeted the exhausted ski party.

It was an evening of lusty eating and grand stories of fun on the piste. Kirsty didn't talk about her hospital visit. Jose's copy lay secret in her bag. She couldn't wait until this trip was over, but persisted with the 'loving it' face and supportive chatter. Forever the actress.

Chapter Twenty-Five

It was several days later that Kirsty caved in. Not that it was a big deal. A pretence that hurt no one. She sidled up to her husband.

'Tom, a word,' Kirsty began, head down rustling in her handbag. 'I know you and the kids enjoyed the skiing trip to France, didn't you?'

'Certainly did; why?'

'Did it ever occur to you to question why I suggested this trip? You know I'm no skier?' Kirsty wasn't finding confession easy.

Tom nestled back in the sofa. 'You needed to get away. You've been under a great deal of pressure. The kids and I wanted you to have some time away from things.' Tom didn't dive into detail. There was no mention of Stephanie or Craig Gayle. No summary of the body in the reservoir and devastating news of her friend's cremation. Old sores don't need rubbing.

'Well,' Kirsty resumed, 'I had another motive that I wasn't quite honest about. My plan was, once you lot were skiing, I could take a trip to the hospital that treated Stephanie, Little Miss Bump, when she had her accident as a youngster on a school trip. I found a resort close by for your leisure and visited the hospital during the day.'

'What?' Tom sat up, a little agitated. 'Why did you do that?'

'I wanted to know. Discover more.' Kirsty gripped her lips

together. 'You probably think I'm round the bend. It was important to me. Some of the details that were just scribbled on the website wall. Everything seemed to be happening far away from me. I wanted to be near to Stephanie.

'So? What on earth could you find out that could uncover how your friend disappeared, that led her to such an awful death?' Tom sat upright, wide-eyed.

'Sit back, and I'll tell you. Not quite news that revealed any surprising eye-openers.' Kirsty related to her grump-faced husband the journey to Hospital Centre Des Escartons and the input of the subterranean archivist, Jose. She attempted to make it sound like a competent enterprise, of hunting down the dusty recluse Jose in his bunker of a vault and extracting vital data; pride in the story of her pursuit.

'We knew about her injuries and how they'd been fixed, and I looked into the disposal of metal from the crematorium furnace. I thought this was enough.' Tom hissed frustrated air. 'So this Jose found the exact details of Steph's treatment after her Alpine accident?' Tom sighed. 'Tell me the gruesome particulars.'

'Seems,' started Kirsty, 'that there were breaks that left her reinforced with metal rods. Steel rod in her leg and some small plate to keep her broken finger straight.' Kirsty couldn't remember the actual name of the metal used. 'I have a few documents that I persuaded Jose to let me copy.' Kirsty left the room and returned speedily with a folder that she shoved into Tom's hand. He wouldn't scan the details until he could be on his own. It was the thoughtful thing to do.

'Well, if you feel there's more to find out,' Tom began, arm encircling Kirsty's shoulder, 'we can always pop over to the Alps next skiing season. I know the kids would enjoy another visit.' He smiled at his own attempt at subtle humour.

When Kirsty had headed for bed, Tom opened the folder that she had smuggled from France. His French was merely a spattering of vocabulary from schooldays long ago. Details of injuries, surgery, medication, procedures were not too difficult to pinpoint with the help of divided layouts and sequences. Tom spent more than an hour perusing the documents and was about to close the folder. His eyes were heavy, and he could hear the soft breathing of his wife. Tantalum. L'acier and tantalum. That's steel for the broken leg and this other stuff for her finger. From heading straight for bed, Tom was reignited. New energy that thrust open his iPad and as quickly onto Google as his machine allowed. Tantalum, chemical element Ta and an atomic number of 73, used to strengthen alloys and other important industrial use. Nothing about it being used medically. The French may not be too fussy about that, he thought. What really caught the tired eyes of Tom Foster was the description of a non-magnetic metal that had a melting point of 3,017 degrees Celsius. Bed beckoned, but Tom's head was buzzing.

It was as if Tom had taken over the crusade. From a supportive husband, he had now picked up the gauntlet and become Kirsty's flagbearer.

Chapter Twenty-Six

Dead ends. It seemed like that to Warren Yates and Paul Leonard. Collins-Maynard and the CPS were sitting on good fresh evidence, but it was fairly obvious there wasn't the energy or the money to pursue Craig Gayle. He'd be just another statistic, another protagonist in an unsolved case. Another battered beige envelope they would have to stow away in the cold case department that neighboured Wimbledon Police Station. Chief Superintendent Collins-Maynard had been on the blower. There wasn't enough for the CPS to juggle the new information, accessible witnesses and for hauling Craig Gayle through the crown court again.

Detective Inspector Warren Yates and Detective Sergeant Paul Leonard were not detecting. They were washing down tea and biscuits, the diet of a real policeman. It wasn't until lunchtime that they pulled down another file to resurrect an investigation that was more than just brown at the edges. There was little enthusiasm. When you get your teeth into an enquiry then any other pile of witness statements, forensic reports, expert testimonies and the inevitable dead end are far from appetising.

It was the newly invigorated Tom who decided to call in on the officers. They were glad for the break. He thought it necessary that Yates and Leonard were aware of Stephanie's repair job in France and his own detective work, and if he could save Kirsty further pain, it would be a bonus.

There wasn't much room in the cramped cold case office. For the two detectives it was tight, but with Tom invited to perch at Warren Yate's desk, genuinely claustrophobic. 'Sorry to intrude,' Tom managed to expel as he squeezed into his snug seat. 'Just wanted to fill you in.'

'Gayle's laughing at us,' Paul Leonard started to explain. 'We know what happened to Stephanie; cremated and crushed, spread in a cloud of dust. Can't touch him. An unreliable witness, foreign hearsay and no forensic evidence. The CPS isn't interested, especially as he's been hauled in front of a crown court already.'

Tom butted in. 'Kirsty has dependable information that might be relevant,' Tom explained. Apparently, when Stephanie was at school she went on the annual skiing trip and ended up in hospital, crashed badly. To help heal injuries, they inserted metal rods. And we know they don't burn. Unfortunately, I have discovered that crematoria, including animal ones, collect any scrap metal left after incineration and sell it off, a regular income, accepted.'

'So we hit another dead end,' Warren Yates interjected.

'She's not letting this go. My wife is determined, and it's a little worrying,' Tom admitted to the two detectives. 'If we could establish a fresh line of enquiry.'

'Some you win and some you lose. That bastard Gayle obviously killed his wife and incinerated her body, but we have our hands tied. I'm not expecting to discover any new evidence that will lead to a successful prosecution,' Warren Yates solemnly told Tom.

'Here's one to hang on to,' Tom began, 'Kirsty established, from the hospital in France, where Stephanie Gayle was treated, that the metal supports for her breakages were not the same type.' Tom bent closer, somewhat intimately, to the two doubting policemen. 'Sure, the main break in her femur was treated with a steel rod used as a splint. But' – Tom paused and focused his eyes on the dubious officers – 'Stephanie's finger break was supported by a small tantalum screw.' Tom swayed back on his perch. The desk rocked slightly.

Both policemen exchanged questioning expressions. Warren Yates gave himself as much room as possible before he spoke. 'Now, Tom, we have little wriggle room with this case, and to be honest we've had to put it to bed already. If you were here with some dramatic fresh evidence, then we could shove everything else aside and renew our efforts. You are giving us nothing. We have told you there are no avenues left. The CPS doesn't want to know, and our chief superintendent won't spend any more money on what he calls a lost indictment. We've tried and used up all our options. Sorry.'

'Hear me out.' Tom pressed forward once again. 'As I've told you, the metal at a crematorium is collected, after the cremation, by a large electro-magnet. These contraptions lift out the steel fragments. They do not attract or extract alloys.' Now he was getting excited. 'Tantalum is an industrial mix that is not magnetic and has a melting point in excess of the capability of any furnace. Surely the small rivet, and I emphasise small, could have been swept up with Stephanie's ashes at Golden Meadows?' Tom rocked back again, lips tightened, stern expression. 'And if it is, then there's the possibility we can locate her scattered remains.'

'As we have said, it's just needles and haystacks,' retorted Paul Leonard, who reacted quickly. 'There's no way Collins-Maynard is going to fund such a time-consuming, and possibly fruitless, search for a sliver of this alloy. Bravo for a fine effort, but it's yet another red herring.'

Tom growled in frustration. 'Each of these splints can be identified. Etched on every piece of metal used to strengthen broken limbs is a number, a unique number. True it would be small, and you'd need more than the naked eye to read it, but surely it would nail Gayle if we found it. Here.' Tom handed the sceptical policemen a copy of the report Kirsty had obtained in France.

'For me, and for you, this seems extremely hopeful, but Collins-Maynard and the rest of the prosecuting ensemble are not going to touch it with a bargepole. The manpower needed is immense, and we have no guarantee we'd find anything.' Warren Yates' eyes drooped soulfully and apologetically.

All three men rested back, the officers in their chairs and Tom against the edge of a wall. In the cloudy silence, Tom was still sizzling. For Kirsty's sake, he was urging a resolution that brought some peace. A difficult task in this crusty little room hanging heavy with distressed beige folders stuffed into the high shelves. Side-lined and sideways shifted into its crow's nest accommodation away from the real policing in the real nick next door. And with occupants to match. A police inspector equally side-lined; worn out and worn down. Worth his own folder in the rack. Alongside was the obligatory black sergeant who, despite his discipline and eagerness, was safer to keep half-hidden high up in an attic nest. Fortunately, he wasn't ready to replace his determined spirit with resignation and kept Warren on his toes.

It was Paul Leonard who eventually broke the sullen silence. 'We have all the evidence that we were able to use in the trial. Now we have at least one witness to state Craig Gayle rented an animal crematorium where we reckon he disposed of his wife Stephanie's body, forensic confirmation that he also murdered Demetrio Nantano, his boyfriend, and lastly the possibility that there is evidence of her final resting place. Stringing all this together and we make little progress. But there is one last throw of the dice.'

Warren and Tom looked enquiringly at the sergeant, who now seemed to be orchestrating proceedings. 'We, and all our force, might well search fruitlessly for a minute piece of metal, yet there is one person who could possibly find it without any problem.' Paul Leonard smiled at the two quizzing faces, pleased with himself.

'Where are we going with this?' queried a sceptical Warren Yates.

'Craig Gayle knows where he scattered Stephanie's remains. Possibly he could find a metal screw, however small.' Leonard studied the two men's gawping gaze.

'He's hardly going to tell us, is he?' Warren Yates almost scoffed.

Paul Leonard offered a smug grin. He was ready with a fine performance. 'If we were to leak this information to Gayle, and that there was the possibility that we could discover its whereabouts and link this scrap of metal to the discarding of his wife's body, he might well be concerned, very concerned,' Paul continued.

'Yeah, but we aren't likely to find it, are we?' interrupted Tom.

'I see your thinking, Paul,' Warren chirped in. 'Gayle could lead us to the evidence. If we were able to ruffle his feathers with this, then Craig Gayle's reaction could include him heading back to where he disposed of Stephanie's ashes to find this tantalum screw, and to destroy this proof of his evil actions.' Warren rested back, and Tom swished this new idea around his head. 'There's a possibility it could work.' Paul had them seriously considering his strategy.

'We are going to have to work out how to leak the existence of this metal screw to Gayle and somehow spur him into leading us to Stephanie's ashes. It is not as easy as it sounds. Collins-Maynard won't okay this unless we have a fool proof plan. Some tight manoeuvres will be necessary.' Paul Leonard rubbed his chin. Once again a silence descended on that cramped room as the three men ran the navigation of this idea through their muddled heads.

'We've already confronted Gayle with the amateur cremation of his wife, and he's just shrugged it off. You can tell that he reckons he's the same as a person who has recovered from a serious virus infection. He feels immune after that fiasco of a trial. Nothing we have is concrete. When we pressed him over the death of Demetrio and the barbecuing of Stephanie, he swiped it away. It's going to be one hard job to stir Craig Gayle into action. He has to feel cornered, hemmed in. He needs to believe the finding of this sliver of tantalum could shatter his story. Could really threaten his freedom.' Warren Yates pulled a crumpled face, distorted by this predicament.

'There are these options. We inform Gayle that this compelling evidence exists and hope he opts to venture off to find it, or we tell him that we've found it already and hope he goes off to check our story. Either way, he leads us to Stephanie's remains and that small metal screw,' Paul Leonard decided.

'Aren't we clutching at straws here?' Tom intervened. 'He probably disposed of his wife's remains where there was no chance of anyone finding them. 'I'm losing faith with this scheme.'

'It's all we've got. It's last chance saloon for us. Every aspect tapers down to this. Yes, we are clutching at straws, because straws are all we have.' Warren Yates stood to signal the end of the discussion. He needed time to think about the next move.

Chapter Twenty-Seven

Craig Gayle was at home, ambling through the caverns of his murky house. His grubby body smelled, and he sported four days of sparse ginger growth around his chins. Not a wholesome man. Ironically there was no sign of a woman's hand or concern about this house. Every room was dark, every curtain edged with grime, every floor gritty, every wall a sad shade of its former colour, every door smudged with handprints. Craig Gayle lived in a shambles of his marital home. Sour and stale air seemed to filter throughout this 1930s building. Upstairs in the sanctuary of their own refuges, the children hunkered down, keeping as separate as they could from the troll of a man who was, in name, their father. Nicholas shielding them safe. Feeding and attending to the needs their mother would have, should have, provided. Probably these children didn't laugh and play like other children of their age. Certainly, their expressions were hostile and often miserable. They had lost their mother, and their father had descended into a tramp-like recluse.

No longer working at New Covent Garden, Craig Gayle bought and sold cars. In his drive and along the road outside was a random selection of middle-aged vehicles. Saloons mostly and of no particular colour. Craig had no appreciation of aesthetics. Deals were done with a grunt and a bundle of cash.

That night Craig Gayle was slumped in a patched leather armchair in the room Stephanie had called the lounge. On a scratched low table next to him was an ashtray piled high with a criss-cross of brown-stained dog ends. Craig dragged heavily on what was left of his present cigarette. And it was in that room, Stephanie's lounge, where she had died. Had been killed. On this occasion, just like many others, he relived that event. His shadowy phantoms were dancing in his head. Every sound, action and emotion. A squalid act. A lonely, bitter man.

Stephanie had been out that afternoon. Pleased to be out. Children swimming. Craig Gayle was waiting; crammed with fizzling anger. It wasn't that he thought Stephanie was seeing someone. He didn't care any more. He and Stephanie were now strangers, but Craig knew this division came at a cost. Craig Gayle was a tight-fisted man. He padded up and down the hallway awaiting her return. He had little idea how his rage would manifest.

There was a good indication of this when Stephanie attempted to sneak into the house; he immediately grabbed her by the shoulders and dragged her into the lounge. No children to form a wall against this snorting man. Stephanie always felt safe when there was a child to cushion any anger. The cape of a matador to quell the bull that Craig often became. Now exposed and being circled by an incensed husband, she held her hands aloft as if they were enough to control such fury.

'I've been to see a solicitor,' Stephanie managed.

'Why?' grunted Craig.

'We can't go on like this. It's enraging you, and it's killing me,' Stephanie began to explain, straightening her flower print dress and sweeping her long brown hair from her brow.

'And what did this solicitor say, tart?' Craig was beginning to bombard Stephanie with abuse.

'We go our own ways. Try not to fight over the kids.'

'You can fuck off with the kids. I'll see them when it suits me,' Craig grumbled. His true colours were being flown. 'Just fuck off out of my life.'

'We will need to divide assets, according to the solicitor,' Stephanie replied as delicately as she could.

'Assets? What fucking assets have you got?' This was shaky ground, and Stephanie knew it. 'All of this is mine. God, I've worked my bollocks off to get this house and build up funds, now some jumped-up shithead tells you we have to share it all. He can fuck off as well.'

Craig stomped around the room, audibly expelling air. 'Listen.' Craig grabbed hold of the cotton floral print dress and pulled Stephanie up to his spitting mouth. 'Listen, you tramp, you are getting nothing, fuck all!'

He held Stephanie tight for a while and slowly let her slide from his grip.

There was a hiatus where both of them looked only at the floor, Stephanie whimpering and Craig seething. Similar sounds, differing reasons.

In his head, Craig Gayle was doing his sums and weighing up the consequences. Careful to concentrate on all he would lose. Miserly and self-centred, he was living a nightmare. And in the tunnel of his darkening thoughts, the only light he could grasp was repeating itself. Around him was the silence of the house with only the swishing noise of passing traffic. Bent over, weak and trembling, was the source of his nagging anxiety. Frail and vulnerable, easy to control, malleable. For what seemed a long time, but was mere minutes, Craig had decided on terrible action.

He approached his quaking wife and lifted her to her full height. Stephanie kept her eyes on the floor, not wanting to look at the monster's face. Tightly he gripped her slumping body, then slipped his gnarled hands furtively from her slim waist up to her neck. Stephanie's full weight being held there. Abruptly, she felt physically threatened. Panic. Her eyes opened like headlights, her lips quivering. Craig Gayle tightened his grip. Felt the loose skin of her neck, thrusting his thumbs into the gristly larynx. Stephanie spluttered; incomprehensible words that spat out. Even tighter the clutch. Stephanie's face reddened, eyes popping, her fingers clawing, scratching at his vice-like hold. Body quaking. Flailing hands. Futile struggle. Craig Gayle's determined grimace, teeth clenched. Shaking out life. Stephanie Gayle's existence on a precipice. No breath. Head hanging. Lifeless, limp. Dead.

Without consideration, Craig Gayle let his wife's body, floral-clad, slide to the floor, crumpled. What had he done? *Shit*, he thought to himself. It had only been half a plan in his mean head. Stop the bleating, hold on to his wealth, truncate the theft. Now the real thinking was necessary. 'He'd come home and found her dead on the floor' – he could make the front door lock appear tampered with. No, there would be the forensic examination of her neck, his prints, DNA and other unseen stuff that would nail him. Craig was sweating. Until he had sorted this out, he needed to move Stephanie's body before the kids came home. Where? Strangulation leaves little trace. A slumped corpse. A corpse that was tricky to hide. Craig racked his brain. Then it dawned. The inspection pit in the garage. Boarded over when not in use. He had stood there; it would easily take a body. A car parked over it. Ideal.

A door led from the kitchen at the back of the house directly into the garage. He pulled up the crumpled doll that had been Stephanie, dress sweeping the floor as he slid her, a guided bent form, through into the garage. A car sat over the well. Craig ventured out the front of the house. A man heavy with guilt. A man imagining everyone who passed knew his culpability. He shunted a parked vehicle up the drive, leaving enough room to drive out the one in the garage perched over the pit, forward enough to expose the well. With jittery hands, he lifted the planks that covered the hollow and contemptibly, with his feet, slid his wife's motionless form, without ceremony, into the examination well. She lay curled and rumpled at the oil-stained bottom until all light was extinguished by the replacing planks. A disguising car reversed to cover it.

Ghosts were spinning as Craig Gayle nervously recalled how, the next day, he had brought home the white Transit van from the market. He would take her somewhere. The river was nearby. The River Mole too shallow, a body easily seen. The Thames too exposed with dog walkers along the towpath. He needed to move fast. His children were asking questions. Where was their mother? When would she be home? Craig was short of answers. Made out that she hadn't returned from a day out and that he too was concerned. Probably stayed with a friend. I'll have a word with her soulmate, Kirsty; she'll know. Anything, any excuse to give him time. If only he had thought this through and discovered the ways of disposing of a body.

It was in the middle of a fitful sleep that the idea came to him. At the market, Steve Bairstow had a massive shredder that would obliterate Stephanie's body without trace, especially with the quantity of other produce he normally gets rid of. No one would notice that all being dumped together.

Craig was always at his stall early, but this day he was there even earlier. He rounded on Steve Bairstow, asked about using the shredder, gave some excuse about a load of rotting melons. Steve was quick to tell him about the need for manning the machine and insistent it required two people, and it would cost him a thousand quid. Money wasn't the problem for once. This needed to be a sole operator. You can't share mangling your dead wife's body with anyone else. Dead end.

Time. It was Craig Gayle's enemy. Stephanie would have to be seen as a missing person, but she wasn't. She lay unmoving in an oily pit in the garage. All his actions robotic, his eyes dilated as a murderer's would be. There was no way he could call the police and report her missing until he had disposed of the evidence. She had been an inconvenience before, and now no change; she had become an alternative nuisance.

Craig called in at a local hostelry, a stepping stone home. Definitely time for a drink. He sat alone in a corner, his thoughts sunk in his glass. It was then that Dean Wallace, another loner, came swaggering in. From the snippets of his conversation and sarcastic banter with bar staff, it appeared that this noticeably slow guy worked at a local pet crematorium. A bright light shone in Craig's head. It could work.

Adopting a chummy persona, name of Dave, he had sidled up to this equally sordid character. Craig began breaking the ice. Chatting about football and buying drinks. Laying a foundation. It would be easier to approach Dean once there was a bonding. Craig let a day pass, when he had anxious kids to placate and a visit to Kirsty Foster. At least he could play at being troubled by his wife's disappearance. Only he knew that murdered Stephanie lay crumpled, stiff and still, glazed eyes in the dimness of the garage.

He met Dean at the same time, after work pint at the Fox and Hounds. Opening up the conversation about his work and prising from Dean his role at Golden Meadows. Now he had to lay it on thick and quick. Dreamed up a tale about having to get rid of animal carcasses urgently, being a farmer like. Offered Dean five hundred quid cash. Knew he wouldn't turn that down. Once he'd secured the deal, he could sever any connection with Dean Wallace, a real numb head.

You don't just use a furnace. Dean Wallace pocketed the dirty money with one grubby hand and with the other scribbled down instructions. To say scribbled would be an understatement, these notes were barely decipherable. Dean was a man of action, not a man of letters. Craig Gayle fidgeted on the spot as if needing a piss. He was aware that his agitation was on display.

Craig Gayle was thinking in a line, one movement at a time. Body, pit, van, furnace, conclusion. All the time fending off a volley of questions from the kids, from Kirsty Foster and assorted neighbours and friends.

Night time or early hours of the morning. All quiet in the house, in the street. He could back up the Transit to the garage doors, but it was too high to get through the opening. Ironically, using a similar faded tarpaulin market cover that he would later use to bind his strangled Portuguese lover, Craig Gayle wrapped his dead wife. Clumsily and without sentiment, he trussed Stephanie in her funeral garb, slid her bent corpse from the inspection pit into, and threaded amongst the junk of his van. Whereas he usually slammed the doors macho shut, this murderer eased them together with merely a click of the locking mechanism. Every move that of a furtive killer. He wouldn't move the Transit beyond the end of the drive. Motoring through the night could well arouse suspicion. For most of the next day, Stephanie Gayle, unknown to her family, was lying in her hearse. No flowers spelling out MUM, or scrum of friends, or glum funeral directors and mourners for her. She was destined for the most unceremonious send-off imaginable.

Later that day, when there was just enough trickle of traffic, Craig Gayle set off. At each corner of his journey, he could hear the weight of Stephanie's body lurching or sliding across the Transit floor and carrying bundles of debris with it. Golden Meadows was closed to visitors, the grounds empty, evening descending, mist drifting eerily amidst the mock-Victorian buildings. Chimney of the crematorium dark, soaring, tallest. Furnace waiting. Craig Gayle backed his van to the doors that Dean Wallace had indicated in his notes. Room to remove a large dog or even a pony, but not easy to slide a roughly packaged dead wife from amidst the trash of a Ford Transit.

Whereas deceased animals could be incinerated together, where each sizzling corpse occupies its own furnace-proof container, Stephanie needed to be eased in as a canvas bundle. Craig Gayle secured the furnace door and studied Dean Wallace's scrawled notes. Buttons and levers, some trial and error. Tense hands followed the erratic notes on the sheet. With first the popping sound of ignition and then the roar of powerful flames, the oven was brought to life. A temperature gauge jiggled at zero and began climbing higher. Through a small triple-glazed inspection window, Craig watched. Watched his victim's form being licked and then engulfed. Stephanie's shroud fizzled and split as heat and flare tore into the wrapping. To Craig Gayle's horror, the tearing flames exposed the ghostly pale of Stephanie's skin as her meagre clothing blackened, flamed, then disappeared. Skin fared no better, and soon that peeled and shredded, organs bubbled and shrunk. Eventually, only the skeletal form of Stephanie Gayle lay in the residues. Craig shivered, not at the sight of his wife's carcass, but at the whiteness and exposure, as if broadcasting his guilt. There was no hiding this evidence. Deliberately Stephanie was shouting out her presence, her fate, her deadness. Craig waited for critical temperatures, for this cremation to be over.

He had not expected the delay. Surely knowing, with any oven, there must be a period of cooling down. Even though Stephanie's bones were cracked and shaved, her skeleton was still advertising her brutal murder. His peering eyes were glued to the glass window. Watching the settling of flake and ash, the crumbling body.

Every move was mechanical. The debris collected within the confines of the furnace. Pulverisation satisfying. Bone crushed and brushed to an even pulp. Swinging into motion a slow-moving magnet, a small metal rod extracted from the pile. Craig knew it was there – holidays, airport security. That was enough history. For a moment, no longer than that, Craig Gayle understood the enormity of his actions, the bizarre cover up and the ludicrous remnants he now handled. His wife was a mere pile of dust. Robotically scrap was removed, and robotically Craig Gayle extracted Stephanie's remains. Heaped in an old cardboard box, it had barely been human; barely been the laughing, giggling, generous human being.

Out of the incinerator doors Craig Gayle stumbled, carrying his boxed-up wife. Out over the threshold. Out in the damp darkness of the Golden Meadows 'garden of remembrance'. Into a wooded area. Even darker there. A concealing darkness. Not a scattering, not a prayer, not a nod of respect. Dumped. Kicked randomly to spread the remains. From the corners of a battered cardboard box, the very last speck of Stephanie Gayle was sprinkled. Rain that peppered the air would slowly disperse a gritty mush that had been Stephanie Gayle.

'She went out in the afternoon,' Craig Gayle began in his call to the local police station. 'And she hasn't returned. It's been three days. Just left the house and hasn't been back. The kids are getting worried, as am I.' Registered as a missing person. He had covered his tracks, he hoped. Now to play it out for his audience and the painful faces of the children. A straight, somewhat anxious expression. No knowledge of her whereabouts, expecting her reappearance anytime. All acted out when the far-from-interested WPC called round to take details. A desperate man, a desperate time.

Stephanie was not returning. Stephanie Gayle was slushy dust, haphazardly sprinkled in a damp copse. Craig Gayle chased the phantoms in his head.

Chapter Twenty-Eight

Warren Yates and Paul Leonard were back at Kirsty's. There were polite greetings and muffled hellos. Statutory tea and biscuits laid out. A policeman's diet.

'You look tired, Kirsty,' observed Warren Yates. 'Probably sick to death with what's been happening, I bet.' The policemen plonked themselves down on the inviting sofa. Tom ventured through the doorway and remained leaning against a wall.

'Is it more bad news or just a courtesy call?' asked Kirsty as she shuffled past the two biscuit-munching officers.

'As you know, we had a session with Tom at the station. It's probably our last chance in this case. We were wondering if you would like to break the news to Craig Gayle about the tantalum sliver that we believe survived the furnace and could be bait to catch Stephanie's killer?' Warren awkwardly suggested. He hadn't worded it well, and he was cursing his lack of tact.

Kirsty sat bolt upright; eyes centred on the inspector. 'If you think, after all that man has put me through, that I could be in his company, let alone talk to him, you must be crazy.' Kirsty was fizzing. 'That shit of a human I would willingly kill. He stole my very best friend and had the hideous impudence to incinerate a beautiful soul. To reduce that perfect individual to ashes, to dust. Crumbled and trashed.' Kirsty slumped back.

Tom was quick to intercede. 'You can't ask her to do this. Not only did Gayle murder her amazing friend, but he also continued to make our lives a misery. Tormenting us. You'd better think of a better plan.'

'We were prepared for Kirsty's reaction to our suggestion. An understandable response.' Warren Yates offered his comforting remarks. 'Paul and I will give our Craig Gayle a visit ourselves. It won't please him; I'm sure he reckons we are persecutors. He might well be right.' Warren smirked. 'It works like this, well we hope it does. Gayle is made aware of the existence of the tantalum screw and how it would have survived any cremation. He, in turn, needs to find the evidence and hurries to Golden Meadows, where we observe him. Haul him in after his treasure hunt, hopefully in possession of the evidence, and he's dug his own grave. Simples.'

'Not sure that's fool proof,' acknowledged Tom. 'I can't see Gayle being easy to dupe.'

'Last chance saloon, I'm afraid. It's all we've got. End of the road here. Stephanie's disappearance has run out of road. If we can trap Gayle, we have a case that the chief super's going to sanction. If we don't, the folder goes to the top shelf of our office. Where no one ever reaches.' Paul Leonard sounded the last post. 'Of course, there won't be any surveillance. Met wouldn't condone the expenditure. We'll rig up cameras.'

'Even more precarious than I thought,' Tom added. 'I hope this will be infrared night vision technology subtly placed; otherwise it's a waste of time.'

'It will be. Don't concern yourself,' Warren assured him. 'Now to plant the seed. We will be off to see Mr Craig Gayle. Wish us luck.'

'Not again. What the fuck do you want?' Craig Gayle was not a man bound by ceremony. Police officers at his door. He didn't like that.

A brace of false smiles. Warren Yates and Paul Leonard were gracious callers. 'Just a word, if that's all right?'

'This is harassment, big time,' Gayle muttered through gritted teeth. 'Haven't you tried every move, every bloody manoeuvre to get me thrown inside?'

'A courtesy call, Mister Gayle. You, of all people, want to know what happened to your wife, don't you?' Paul Leonard smoothly stroked Gayle's ego. 'We have a small matter we would like to discuss that could lead to solving this mystery, once and for all.'

Gayle wasn't going to invite these policemen in. That was the plan until the road outside seemed alive with onlookers, neighbours shuffling past and a scrum of kids. Reluctantly he ushered Warren and Paul into the kitchen. It stank. It stank of old dinners and burnt cooking. It stank of spilled milk and rancid butter. It stank of him. Gone were fastidiously swabbed sides and a wife's pride in neatly racked larder and arranged refrigerator, the surgical whiff of bleach and spray cleaners and the care and pride of a woman. It was a hole of tumbling pots and scored surfaces, of greasy dishes and puddled leftovers. Windows streaked and stained floor.

'What?' Gayle gruffly managed, his back to the officers. 'What is so fucking important you need to come round here disturbing my peace, the kids' peace?'

'You will remember that the last time we spoke, we informed you of evidence from our source that took us to conclude your wife, Stephanie, had been murdered and her body disposed of in an incinerator. Burned by you at a location we have yet to discover, but we will,' Warren Yates officially informed him.

'Absolute nonsense,' Gayle growled. 'If you're so sure,

then why aren't you arresting me?' Craig fussed around the kitchen, seeming to busy himself but really doing nothing. 'I can't believe I'm being hassled yet again. You are knocking on the wrong door.'

'Are you aware that your wife was involved in a skiing accident when she was at school, Mr Gayle?' Paul Leonard asked.

'What?' It took time for Gayle to fall in line. 'Yeah, I knew.'

'And her breakages strengthened with metal inserts and screws?'

'Yeah.' Gayle responded. He could see where this was moving, but he also knew they were going to make no headway with this line of enquiry. He had made sure of that.

'When a body is incinerated, certain articles, usually manmade items, are extracted from the final ashes that are potted for the family. Of course, it's basically crushed bone and no more; the victim's flesh and clothing totally destroyed in the heat.' Paul was trying to nudge Craig Gayle into remembering the horrors of his performance at the crematorium.

Of course Gayle was recalling, through some tight mental mesh, that event, but he was reminded of his tidying up job at Golden Meadows; the magnet and the steel pin so easily removed. A wild goose chase by the police officers. 'So what's this all about? Nothing you've been saying has any relevance to me.' Gayle was ready to show them the door.

'Now, here's an interesting facet of cremation that you might be fascinated by,' Paul Leonard began. 'Although pacemakers are removed, yes, even from dogs, and steel used for limb repairs taken from the final ashes, there are metals that either do not melt or are not magnetic that survive the furnace temperature. They are a group of alloys perfected by man.'

'So?' Craig Gayle impatiently rubbed his knees and chewed his tongue. How did it concern him?

Paul shuffled in his chair closer to Gayle, penetrating his lacklustre eyes with a piercing stare. 'So, your wife, Stephanie Gayle, not only had her femur repaired after the skiing accident, with a steel rod, she also had a finger held in place using an alloy called tantalum. This very small, probably unnoticeable, support would have, if she had been cremated, survived the incineration. And, more importantly, could go overlooked in the haste of amassing the final ashes. So easy for a frantic man to miss as he swept up his dead wife's charred remains. Stuck in the globular lump scraped out of the oven. A nervous rashness in the hurry to stay unobserved. Most likely this sliver of tantalum lies, along with her dust, in her final resting place.' Paul pulled back and surveyed the room. 'Is this a resting place that you know of, and can take us to, Mr Gayle?'

Whizzing around his head, Gayle attempted to understand what he had just been told. The two detectives watched. Gayle was breathing hard, audibly. 'As I've said already, this does not concern me.' Deeper, louder breathing. 'Now. If you don't mind, leave me alone and fuck off. You ain't going to pin this on me. No, never.' His words rambled out with his heavy breath. Gayle struggled to stand and shambled towards the kitchen door, hand gesticulating to indicate the policemen's departure.

'Do not worry, Mr Gayle, we will be looking ourselves for this piece of alloy, and when we find it, we'll be back. You can be sure of that,' Warren snarled.

Even a disoriented man has the capacity to avoid elephant traps. There was no way they would know where to look. The garden of remembrance at Golden Meadows was vast, and ashes had been deposited in every corner for a long time. Gayle didn't speak to the detectives as he threw open the front door. Muddling along in his head was his next move. Were they having him on, throwing him bait, about this piece of tantalum? Was he supposed to rush to the crematorium and dig around for this condemning item of evidence? Surely they wouldn't expect him to charge off merely on their dubious information? No, it's all a ploy; they've got nothing new.

Gayle was about to trundle back to his kitchen when the doorbell sounded. Whoever it was rang twice. 'Yes,' Gayle muttered before fully opening the door, only to find the two officers returned to the doorstep. He stepped back, baffled.

'Sorry, Mr Gayle,' explained Paul Leonard, 'I forgot to leave this with you.' Paul pulled a crisp sheet of A4 from his briefcase. 'It's a copy of the original French hospital report of your wife's accident in the Alps. We didn't want you to think this was all a story. No, you will read an account of exactly what we have told you. Happy reading.' With that, the two policemen moved briskly down the front path.

Chapter Twenty-Nine

Warren Yates held his tea mug more firmly and clutched his digestive biscuit almost to breaking point. 'Now we wait.'

'I can't see that Gayle will start rushing to Golden Meadows anytime soon, if ever,' Paul Leonard added.

'I'm setting up a few surveillance cameras. There's no way Collins-Maynard will sanction officers in attendance, a stakeout. I know we are on a fishing trip, but it's all we've got.' Warren sat with his tea dribbling on the worn carpet floor. 'I'm sure we unsettled Gayle enough to start him wriggling.'

And Warren was correct. Craig Gayle was more than wriggling; he was squirming. He knew of Stephanie's injuries as a girl, and he was more than a mere witness to the disposal of the steel rod at the furnace that had strengthened her femur. The police hadn't handed him a fake hospital report; they daren't. Sure enough, the small repair of her finger was enabled using this alloy, tantalum. He wasted no time searching for details of the metal. He rubbed his fingers, and his legs shook as he realised the importance of this sliver that he must have easily overlooked in the cardboard box of ashes that had been his wife. Gayle stood and stamped his feet in anger and frustration. It had been watertight until now. His next step rumbled through his thick head.

If you place out your snare, you have to know it will be taken and persuade your prey to visit that location. Craig Gayle knew there was no way he was going to lead the fucking coppers to the last resting place of his incinerated wife. He wasn't an idiot. Warren Yates, wily and experienced, yet outwardly congenial and just an average Mr Plod, was a pace ahead of Gayle. In his morbid cave of a living room, Craig Gayle was sieving through ideas, channelling possible actions. He couldn't rest until this loose end was well and securely tied. No interfering copper was going to catch him. They would be watching him, waiting for him to give away the last resting place of his wife. Scowling in and around his grubby house and making short and winding trips, Gayle eventually concluded the hounds were not sniffing near him. Yet, he would wait. Trailing and tailing him was beyond the meddling policemen. He would make a move; one that the police weren't expecting, but one that Warren Yates was waiting for.

The Fox and Hounds was a tasteless pub that was filling up with an assortment of manual workers who rounded off their weekly efforts with several pints, swigged along with some disgusting jokes they couldn't tell at home. Craig Gayle slid in. Sure that the police had become aware of the incineration of his wife, he now regretted his loose tongue during his sexual activity with Nantano. Nothing else. There was no mention of when and where he had burned her. No mention of Dean Wallace or Golden Meadows. If they had known, if Wallace had grassed him up, they would have been biting at his heels.

Dean Wallace was on parole and picked up casual work needing brawn, not brain. When he swaggered into the pub, he wasn't expecting to find Craig Gayle seated near the fruit machine. It was as if heat from his body was rising inextricably around his neck and filling his head. Dean rushed to find his own corner. Here was the guy he had snitched to the law. Was he there to wreak revenge, brutally, like he did to his wife? His legs twitched under the table, head hovering above his beer.

Craig Gayle approached gingerly, and Dean pretended not to notice. Gayle sat, cornering Dean, who supped and avoided eye contact. Each harbouring engrained mistrust.

'Didn't need this,' Gayle began furtively, trying to shield his mouth inside the lapels of his coat, 'but need your help again.'

Dean faced him. Blank and stupid. As if no recognition, or feigning an attempt to identify his table guest. 'Sorry?' Dean mumbled.

'Remember me?' Gayle snapped.

Dean Wallace tried to smuggle his identity behind a rough woollen scarf. Of course he did recognise Craig Gayle or Dave. You don't forget helping your local killer. 'Yeah, suppose I do.' A degree of reassurance. Gayle wasn't blasting him for blabbing to the law.

'It's an earner. More than our last arrangement. A grand in it for you.' Gayle almost choked on the amount.

Dean Wallace had been hoping this encounter would be over quickly, that Gayle would go away, but now he was all ears. There wasn't much Dean wouldn't do for one thousand pounds. Both men looked around as if expecting watching eyes. The pub was sparsely filled, and none of the other drinkers were the least bit interested in the grubby couple who swapped whispers in a scrum at the far end of the bar. 'Been inside, can't get hold of the oven keys now. Wouldn't be able to get you in there.'

'Don't need that again. Just want you to find something for me,' Gayle garbled.

'Find something?' Dean was keeping hold of the one thousand in his head. Puzzled at that moment by what Gayle was saying. 'Find what?'

'When I was at the furnace,' Gayle began, 'I dumped

something with the animal remains.'

Animal remains? thought Dean, the remains of his fucking dead wife. What's he after?

Craig Gayle was having difficulty. He'd supposedly incinerated dead animals, and now he was offering the furnace man one thousand pounds for a simple errand. It was difficult not to sound suspicious.

Dean Wallace was finding it awkward to deal with. He was well aware of what Gayle had used the crematorium for, yet it would seem Gayle himself was in the dark about this, unaware Dean Wallace knew the truth behind his incineration, and he had no idea that Dean had spoken to the Old Bill. 'So, Dave, you want me to find something you chucked away when you used the Golden Meadows furnace? Got to be valuable, offering me a grand to find it.' Not so dumb, Dean Wallace. Calling Gayle Dave without correction helped both men to twitch less.

Craig Gayle had not come unarmed. Even a desperate man has a plan. 'Dropped it near the trees there when I was discarding stuff. It is a small metallic mechanism non-corroding, bearing my foreign bank safe storage box details etched onto it. So very small, I hadn't realised I had lost it.' Craig Gayle thought that was enough to satisfy his dense companion. 'Just between us. I don't want this broadcast. Security and all that.' Even to Dean Wallace, it was all transparent. He didn't even question the length of time Gayle had been without his precious bank box details. 'One grand if you find it. No shit.'

Gayle pinpointed the small copse where the remains of Stephanie Gayle were sprinkled, described as best he could imagine the appearance of this metal sliver, reiterated the delicious reward of one thousand quid and scrawled down a phone number.

Chapter Thirty

Two men were busy. Dean Wallace's cloudy mind was working out when would be the best time to start rummaging through the undergrowth at Golden Meadows, Warren Yates travelling up to Imperial College. Both on designated expeditions.

Dean Wallace still had his Golden Meadows' gate key and high-viz jacket. Less conspicuous even when the crematorium was officially closed. Along with a faded baseball cap, dark jeans, old boots, scarf and scavengers' gloves, he was in uniform for a forager, a skulking retriever. He couldn't wait. Gayle's bullshit about bank details didn't even fool Dean's gullible noddle, but for one thousand pounds, he would appear to swallow any story.

Meanwhile, Warren, in London, meandered around the remaining puddles from the previous night's showers, past The Albert Hall, rotund and spectacular, on his way to meet his nephew, who was in his second year at Imperial. Flitting near him were clusters of camera-wielding tourists. London University was a milestone for the Yates' dynasty, as no one had achieved such a high education as young Oliver Yates. Being taken out for lunch was a real treat for an undergraduate, even if he did have to converse with his dull uncle. They were meeting at a small Italian place not far from the College, and hopefully, they would have an outside table so that Oli could be seen by envious passing students. Flaunt it.

Dean waited until he knew Golden Meadows would be

shut. The high, metal-spiked gates almost a portcullis entrance to this animal disposal site so quaintly titled. He made little sound; there was a silvery moonlight that cast sinister shadows across the 'garden of remembrance', and Dean had brought his faithful torch. In no time, he was at the small thicket carefully described by Craig Gayle, his flashlight beams prodding the darkness and flicking with every move the shadowy figure of the explorer made.

Warren dined his nephew, as he wished, on an outdoor table with only the occasional visit of annoying pigeons, their eyes on Oli's pastrami-littered pizza. Oliver was surprised by his uncle's probing questions and an unusual interest in his progress. Not such a dreary relative. Warren Yates was in the autumn of his police career; no doughnut, but sharp and inventive. Oliver underestimated his uncle, but before they left their table, he was well aware that this lunch invitation was not born out of kinship.

By the time Dean Wallace left Golden Meadows, the sun was threatening to rise, birds finding their voice. How he had searched. Nothing. All he could picture was the toppling pile of notes making a thousand pounds. And when at home asleep, all that he could picture was that same pile burning away in front of him. Dean Wallace hadn't noticed the two fresh cameras that had picked up his bowed figure scuttling towards, and returning from, the open gardens of the crematorium. Not recognisable to the unremarkable observer, yet clearly their furnace man snitch, Dean Wallace, to Warren and Paul. Little was Dean aware of the questions that would be aimed in his direction once the pictures were downloaded. He would visit again. Dean was determined he was going to hold on to the money.

'Shit!' exclaimed Warren Yates. It didn't take long for the

scruffy form of Dean Wallace to be identified. 'It's Wallace. Recognise him anywhere. What the hell is he doing there?' Paul Leonard rushed to the screen to watch the furtive movements of the treasure hunter. 'Do you reckon he's the errand boy and that he's found it? We need to watch him if he's going to carry it home to Gayle.'

'Of course,' Warren continued, 'Gayle's henchman. Craig Gayle wasn't going to show his face at the crematorium, so he's got the resident Dumbo to do his dirty work for him. And it looks like he hasn't been successful, seeing as he was there till the early hours.' Both officers sat back to consider their options. Warren was more assured than his junior policeman. 'It's moving our way,' Warren added. Paul Leonard scratched his head, quite unsure of a next move. 'We wait for few days and then we haul Wallace in, Paul. We are starting to move forward in this case. Cameras show he was at Golden Meadows far too long to have found the metal sliver, so he'll very likely be back. Dean Wallace wouldn't be squirrelling around for nothing.'

Dean Wallace was a terrier and a retriever. Terriers dig for hours, and retrievers never give up. Yes, he hadn't found anything but that could have been down to poor directions or navigation. He would return. A rudimentary message to a displeased Craig Gayle confirmed his dogged approach and a determination to scour the copse area totally. You don't let money like that slip away. He'd got his teeth into this assignment.

Same uniform, same identifiable bowed frame. Dean Wallace moved through the ornamental cast iron gates and slithered to his hunting ground once again. God knows what clogs of ash he sieved through this time. Although he was sure he was dealing with the remains of Stephanie Gayle, he could well be sifting the remnants of any deceased hound or rabbit. You can recognise animals from humans in life, but once they've kicked the bucket and have been torched, there is no telling them apart. And from mound upon mound of anonymous remains, Dean Wallace rummaged. His ragged trousers were covered in a white slurry of gooey ash when his body told him it was time to waddle away from the crematorium, again defeated. He wasn't prepared for the greeting he received as he eased the gates shut.

Warren Yates and Paul Leonard had watched their scurrying searcher arrive at Golden Meadows. It was time to haul him in. At the gates, they quickly surrounded Dean and ushered the terrier into the rear of their car. Both playing the 'good cop'.

'What you doing?' Dean gasped. 'I ain't done nothing wrong.'

'Easy, Dean, just want to have a little chat.' Warren, who had sat in the back of the car with Dean, offered him a cigarette, not that Warren was a smoker of this cheap brand; this packet was just part of his armoury. Given to villains as a token. There weren't many who declined and that were ready to explain the ill-health perils of smoking. This packet had been open for a long time, and Warren had no way of knowing if the fags were stale. Dean rested back and took a lengthy audible intake of smoke that seemed to stay in his lungs for a dangerously long time. 'So what were we up to in the crematorium? Didn't think you worked there any more. And, if my watch is right, it's gone three in the morning. Strange behaviour, you'll agree.' Warren could see Dean Wallace struggling for an answer behind the lingering cloud of tobacco smoke.

Paul Leonard leaned back from the driver's seat, inches

from Dean's face. 'And we know it's not the first time you've been exploring the crematorium. CCTV cameras have picked you up, scavenging around until the early hours. You're on a mission Wallace, aren't you?'

'Looking for some of my stuff that I'd left there,' mumbled Dean. It was weak and far too thin for the police to contemplate it. He hadn't prepared, and it was probably beyond his ability at any time.

Time for sarcasm, even at that early hour. Paul Leonard, wide-eyed. 'And what stuff was that, Dean? Your favourite shovel, wellington boots or an animal corpse? We aren't fucking stupid. You're wasting police time. Are we going to have to take you down to the station and squeeze you till you pop, because pop you will? Let's stop arsing about and come clean.'

Squirm and bluster were Dean's efforts to shake off the Old Bill. Old Bill wasn't budging. You don't let go of a thousand quid that easily. Warren and Paul waited, watched their prisoner wriggle and fidget, and listened to more futile excuses for his visit to Golden Meadows. Another two cigarettes and a few threats of prosecution for trespass and withholding information later, and Dean Wallace was ready to raise the white flag.

'Looking for something someone lost, I was,' Dean muttered.

'And who was that someone?' Warren chirped, giving away his relief that Dean was spilling the beans once again.

'Just a bloke who reckons he'd dropped something when he were there,' Dean weakly answered.

'Come off it, Dean, we all know who sent you scrabbling through all that mush and shit of the crematorium,' Paul Leonard snapped. 'It was Craig Gayle, wasn't it?'

'Yeah.' Dean leaned forward, rocking slightly where he sat. 'And what did our wife-killer want you to look out for at the crematorium?'

Dean watched the thousand quid turn to vapour as he succumbed to the pressure of a police interrogation. 'Some piece of metal. Said it was bank details. Knew it weren't, but there were money in it, you see.'

'We see, Dean. You weren't lucky in your search, and you reckon the money's gone the same way, don't you?' Warren Yates sat closer, stale smoke still loitering near their villain. 'Here's the deal, Dean. To get you out of this mess, you go through the rooting process again at the crematorium tomorrow and let us know if you find anything. Keep Gayle informed and arrange to meet him at the end of the week. If you listen to me, you could still keep the dosh. I will explain more tomorrow.' Warren leaned towards Dean as if whispering covert strategies.

Paul Leonard screwed up his face, unsure of his fellow officer's reasoning. He ushered Warren from the vehicle. 'What's that for? Why the Gayle rendezvous?'

Warren Yates was holding back a wry smile. Paul could sense something amiss. 'We'll get here and take our grimy furnace man down the station when he leaves tomorrow. I have a feeling we could seal this case if we play it guardedly.'

'What have we got? A scavenging man finding nothing, a wife-killer who will get away and a lot of our time chasing ghosts.'

'Faith, Paul, faith.' Paul Leonard had never seen Warren so buoyant. 'I have a scheme up my sleeve. All will be revealed when we get this tyke down the nick. Believe me.' And with that, he jumped back in the police car and declared they were escorting Dean back to his vehicle, which he had dumped out of sight down a neighbouring road.

Chapter Thirty-One

Oliver Yates was perched ornamentally at the same table as before. He had already ordered himself a Peroni as he felt he deserved it. Bottle held at the neck, cross-legged leaning back, smirking at the other students passing. Why not display this temporary affluence? Uncle Warren would soon be there. Twice in a week, lunch with a relative he had hardly seen during the last three years. Of course there was purpose in Warren's generosity.

Uncle Warren Yates was late, a policeman's unpunctuality. It had been a late night, further extended with an explanation to keep Paul Leonard happy. Now he was walking against the low sunlight that blinded him on occasions as the beams shot through the gaps in the buildings. Central London was a maze where he wasn't lost but where he wasn't comfortable. Smartly dodging what seemed wave after wave of office workers and jabbering tourist groups.

'Hi, Unc,' was Oliver's greeting. Warren was unimpressed by his nephew's confident welcome. He only broke his frown with a quick smile as he jerked a chair from the table and sank down. 'You look frazzled,' Oliver added as his uncle slumped back.

'Trains late, me tired, people ambling aimlessly, traffic puffing shit into the atmosphere. Just another day in a policeman's life,' a resigned uncle announced. 'At least you look settled.'

A waiter interrupted their discussion. Oliver was eager to order, Warren more thoughtful as he looked down at his buttons tightening on an expanding belly. He would keep to the bruschetta while his nephew chose to be stocked up with a giant, loaded pizza. Another beer and a gelato, laidback gloating, Ollie could nestle back into his chair, even thinking about a nap.

Warren broke the post-meal silence. Leaning across to his nephew and lowering his voice. 'Everything go okay? I will need to get back to the station; work to do.'

Oliver lifted his lounging body and delved deeply into his jeans pocket, pulling a folded brown envelope. Trying to conceal the move, similar to a spy handing over a grubby secret, Oliver pushed it into Warren's hand. Who quickly slipped it furtively into his own pocket. 'Thanks. I will be in touch. Mum's the word.' With that, Warren held his forefinger to his lips and winked. He was off. Oliver would rest on his laurels and stroll back to the College in his own time. He was proud of his work, especially how tricky it was to etch, on that mere scrap, as his uncle had instructed, the barely visible inscription.

Warren cruised home. A sparsely filled District Line train that trundled and waddled along, pausing at every station before its terminus at Wimbledon. Mid-afternoon and the office workers were deskbound, and the tourists, like ants, were filing into museums and galleries. Every now and again, he would feel into his pocket to touch the crumpled brown envelope, and in that, every now and again, he would trace in his head the forthcoming tactics that momentarily lit up his usually dour expression.

Paul Leonard was waiting. 'We best set off if we hope to meet up with Dean Wallace,' he told the inspector as he arrived back at the station, or should we say the attic room in a building next to the police station.

Dean was waiting for them in the shadows, dusty and disgruntled. Another venture into his garden of remembrance that he'd like to forget. Like the naughty boy of the class, Head stooped, motionless, empty-handed.

'We need to take him somewhere quiet, probably to our office; yes, it'll be empty now,' Warren Yates mumbled in part to himself, but enough to be heard. 'Get him in the car, Paul.'

During the journey, Dean was bemoaning a lost cause and how he had scoured what he thought was every inch of the grounds of Golden Meadows without success. Again he saw the thousand quid disappearing over the horizon. The two policemen listened without comment. Dean smelled of soil, damp ash and foliage; he was grimy and dishevelled. You wouldn't have him in your own car. A police car had witnessed the like before. Still, both officers ensured the windows were wound down.

Tea was the only offering back in the confined room, high in the building next to the main station in Wimbledon, and, of course, a saucer of digestives. It meant sitting closer than the two officers liked. 'Look a bit dejected, Dean. No luck again,' Paul confirmed with half a smile.

'Nah, I'm seeing Gayle tomorra night, and it ain't goin' to be a nice time,' Dean gurgled through his tea.

'Well, we have some good news for you, Mr Wallace, which could brighten your day,' Warren announced. 'When things appear difficult, when plans finish with a dead-end, there's often someone to step forward to offer solace and solution. And my dear Dean, it is me. I am your saviour. Just do as I say, and it will all be back on track.' Warren stroked his pocket, rustling the crumpled brown envelope.

'Yeah,' Dean replied without a hint of relief or enthusiasm. Paul Leonard, too, was far from convinced things were on the up.

'We want you to meet up with Craig Gayle as planned. Tell him you've found the small metallic sliver he was looking for, and you want your reward. No, you play a different game. You have what he wants, and you proceed to inform him that you are well aware of the real reason he was so concerned about retrieving this missing alloy shard. Take the upper hand. Expose his animal incineration lie. Lay it on thick; keep nagging him about his nasty deed. Remind him of his cremated wife. Pursue it. Ask for double the amount. Demand two grand.' Warren Yates was relishing his moment.

'Easy, Inspector,' Paul Leonard interrupted. 'Aren't we jumping the gun here? Gayle will see through this tale.' He pulled Yates aside and into the hallway. 'Where's the leverage here? It's no good telling Gayle that the tantalum screw has been found and expecting him to crack. He's not falling for that fake news.'

'Faith. Rest assured; my deception has legs. It should work. Keep listening,' Warren soothed.

On their return, Dean was still in the process of buying Warren's plan. Tongue-tied and a little confused. 'But, I haven't found his piece of bloody metal,' came a strangled response.

Having a nephew, a bright one at that, who had enrolled in an Engineering Alloys course at Imperial College, has its uses and its rewards. Warren pulled out the scrunched brown envelope. Merely occupying a rumpled corner was a tiny piece of metal. Warren pinched it out with his thumb and forefinger, held it up to the light and passed it to Dean. Precious. 'We found it right at the beginning. That's why you had no luck.' Warren tried to sound convincing. Paul Leonard could not believe what was happening and was struck dumb. 'Now you have your pot of gold. This minute alloy gets you your prize. However, all this does not come without conditions. We will let you keep the money. I am sure Gayle will come across with the two thousand quid. We get our man. Here's what happens. As I said, you dangle this in front of Gayle and demand the extra cash. He is desperate for the tantalum screw and will come up with the cash. Hopefully, in the negotiations, Gayle relates the real story behind your find.'

Dean could not stop twiddling the alloy in his hand, turning and studying the tiny particle that he had rummaged through scorched remains to find. The coppers had had it all the time. For a moment, he felt used and a victim. 'Anything else, protection? Ain't much use to me, two grand, if that Gayle repeats what he done to his missus and that foreign bloke. No stranger to killing.'

'Dean, you will not be alone. Well, as you will soon discover, there is the necessity to wire you. No clumsy technology. Devices are subtle these days, just a small mic and a few wires. Won't feel a thing. We, an instant task force, will be listening and ready to react at speed. Guaranteed safety. No worries.' Warren was making pledges that Collins-Maynard would never sanction.

Paul Leonard was statue-still. Speechless. He couldn't believe what he was hearing. Had his mentor, Inspector Warren Yates, just broken one of the basic rules of the Force? Falsifying evidence was a leftover from the 1970s, when it wasn't unusual for officers wishing to accelerate a sound arrest to slip a dubious substance into a known criminal's pocket.

Expeditious method commonly used. When Paul finally regained his voice, he dragged Warren aside, closed in on his face and spat out his disbelief at his inspector's action. 'What the hell? You've told him we found this fucking piece of metal. We didn't. Where did you get that from?' It was an interrogation. Paul couldn't stop shaking.

'I understand, Paul. Just listen. We weren't going to find the real one. It was obvious. Dean wasn't going to have any luck either. This is the final furlong for me. I am a remnant hanging out for retirement. I need to tie up loose ends. Kirsty Foster needs closure.' Warren Yates shrugged his shoulders, which said *it's with reluctance but ultimately necessary*. Leaving Dean in the office, there was only the corridor for this exchange. Warren closed in on Paul and held his shoulder in a fatherly way. 'I don't know if I've mentioned it before, but my sister's boy is a student at Imperial, studying materials. Not my cup of tea. However, he's interested. Bright lad. And his very naughty uncle got him to produce our tantalum sliver, our finger-strengthening screw. Our only physical evidence to ensnare our wife-killer. I know it was a feckless idea. I was desperate. We both were desperate. I'd had enough of brick walls.'

Paul was still tumbling this new situation around his tangled head when the two policemen sauntered back into the poky room. Dean Wallace hadn't moved. He was still toying with the very small bit of tantalum. Such a minute piece of dull alloy, Paul thought, yet such an explosive potential. Dean could visualise it only as a pile of notes, notes that now amounted to two thousand quid.

'Get here tomorrow afternoon, and we'll wire you up. It's no big deal. Just a simple piece of kit,' Warren explained, knowing it needed to be undemanding for uncomplicated Dean Wallace. 'I'll take that. You'll have it tomorrow.' Warren picked the tantalum sliver from Dean's hand.

Dean arrived the next day as planned. The two officers were quick to get their lure primed and ready for action. 'Shirt off, Dean. Strip to the waist,' encouraged Paul Leonard. He soon wished he hadn't. As Dean Wallace removed his clothing, a warm stale aroma from his lily-white body seemed to fill the room. Dean was not one for regular cleanliness. There was a distinct blackness in parts, and a sickly stench of body odour from his matted armpit hair. Even he was embarrassed. Dean's skin was otherwise very pale, and his chest hair wiry and sparse. A small, but growing, tummy hung over his greasy trousers. Scrawny arms with evidence of a rash and other ugly spots. A stinking mess of a man.

Warren felt like pinching his nose as he approached the reeking torso. He wished he had gloves. From a small cardboard pack, Warren pulled out some small wires, tiny plastic discs and a roll of tape. Identifying where he was going to locate the device, he lifted Dean's arm slightly, tore off a piece of tape with a distinctive ripping sound of relieving adhesion, and positioned the first post, much to the discomfort of the human bait. It was almost clinical, much like an ECG setup. Dean lifted and lowered his arms as Warren Yates fitted him up; in more ways than one.

'Ain't comfortable. You sure we need this? Won't Gayle suspect?' Dean muttered as he pulled on his grimy clothes.

Warren didn't answer. Eyes only on this task. 'The switch is in your pocket. A simple press and it's on,' Warren demonstrated and explained. 'Don't change your clothes, and make sure nothing gets loose. I don't want to go through this again.' It was putting the detective off his food, and Dean Wallace wasn't going to even think of a clothes swap. He never did. 'When you meet Gayle, switch on the device. We will be listening not far away. Tell him that on your last visit, you were scrambling around and found the piece of metal so valuable to him. Don't hand it over right away. Put him straight, build up the approach; tell him how you are aware of what he had used the crematorium furnace for. Tell him bluntly that you know he had hideously burned the body of his dead wife. Then you raise your demands. Wave, not too close, the small alloy screw that had held his wife's finger together and survived the inferno. It is the only physical evidence, and you have it. Make him grovel.' Warren massaged his snare with a low, almost whispered, explanation. 'Craig Gayle won't be expecting this wire. He won't have realised we are involved. Simply play it relaxed. An easy exchange. Keep that fresh pile of crisp notes firmly lodged in your head.'

Chapter Thirty-Two

The Fox and Hounds was far from busy. Late afternoon before builders and a variety of other manual workers finished off their day, downing jovial pints over raucous discussion that centred on the recent Premiership games. Craig Gayle collected a drink and found an empty table, a quiet corner. He was a toxic mixture of anxiety and frustration, smaller and bent over as if older. Each movement, scuffing his chair, lifting his beer, jerky and rigid. His breathing more snorting and pig-like. Eyes that flickered and darted. Where was that twat, Wallace?

Dean Wallace breezed into the pub. Easy money can make even the dullest individual sparkle. He whipped out the chair from beneath the table and plonked himself down with his paymaster.

'Why so happy?' Craig Gayle groaned meekly.

'Got it,' Dean Wallace announced, face lit and beaming. Boy done good. Top of the class. A delving hand into his pocket switched on the listening device.

Suddenly, Craig Gayle changed. Bolt upright, eyes alight. A fresh expectancy, a pricked alertness. 'You have?' he bumbled. Gayle pulled his chair closer. Dean Wallace eased back. 'Show me,' demanded the revitalised scruff.

'I'm not stupid,' Dean uttered as he backed off out of Gayle's reach. He opened a cupped hand with the smallest of metallic pieces deep in his palm. 'Exactly what you were after, I believe.'

Gayle glared into Dean's open hand at the merest splinter that was dull like pewter or aluminium. His breathing heavier. Almost there. Dean's grinning face above. Gayle lifted his gaze and stared, owl-eyed into the crazed visage.

'Give it over,' demanded Craig Gayle.

'Remember the deal, Mr Gayle,' Dean responded.

Craig Gayle was more than a little bewildered that Dean used his name. Shrugged off the surprise. Yes, he well remembered the offer, but, as usual, was loath to part with any cash. From inside his tatty jacket, he pulled a tight wad of fifty-pound notes, held together with an elastic band. Dean's eyes lit up at once. Avoiding any spectators, half hidden by the table, Craig counted out twenty notes. And checked and counted them again. Like a dog with a bone, he held on tightly to the money.

'Hand it over then,' Gayle hissed.

Dean Wallace wasn't letting go of his treasure that easily and stood his ground. Tightening his grip on the tantalum screw, he pulled his chair closer to the angry face of Craig Gayle. Dean's face uncomfortably near. A man on a mission.

'Ain't no secret, Gayle. I know you fucking destroyed your wife's body in my furnace. Fucking story about disposing of diseased animals was shit. Think I'd fall for that. No, reducing her body to ash was your only purpose for using the furnace at Golden Meadows.' Laser eyes fixed on Craig Gayle's pale face. 'Methinks my find is worth more than a crummy thousand quid.' Dean's face cracked into a smile. 'If this bit of metal saves your bacon, then I think we can double the prize. Don't you? Two grand, mate.' Dean rubbed his hands together, teeth bared, lips widened. Delighted.

It was like lighting a fuse. Dean eased back as he felt and saw Craig Gayle building up steam. His face reddened, and his eyes were ready to pop. Half raised from his seating position, he exploded. In a voice that seemed to come from a cellar inside his body, the low hiss announcing the detonation of his anger.

'Two thousand fucking quid?' Craig loudly sucked in more air. 'The deal was a grand, and that's all you're goin' to get. Now let me have the piece of metal.'

Dean stood his ground, despite some lower body quivering. 'No, mate. I can recognise you're a desperate man. You pay up. Two thousand and we'll call it a day.'

More steam. Heavy intakes of the pub's stale air. Gayle leaned forward, reaching out, he managed to grab Dean by his saggy neck, jerking him over the table towards his spluttering mouth. A face of pure fury. 'No one double-crosses me. Nobody sucks me arid, steals my money,' puffed Gayle. 'My fucking wife tried that one, tried to squeeze me dry.' Craig Gayle was losing it. Saliva was visibly bursting in spray off his lips. He pulled Dean even closer, inches from his face. 'So I squeezed the fucking life out of her. And that's just what I'll do to you if you try to swindle me.' Fast breathing and fizzing panting, still clinging to Dean Wallace, tensing his hold with every hissing breath.

Outside, squad car-bound, they had heard enough. Warren Yates and Paul Leonard were on their feet, skipped out of the surveillance vehicle, leaving coffee still curling steam and sandwiches half eaten; cartoon teeth marks of a disturbed snack. Hurling their bodies through the double doors of the pub, they quickly spotted Craig Gayle clutching on to Dean Wallace as if strangling the furnace man. Regulars and coarse builders, who were filing in, started back. They had things to hide but not worthy of a police raid.

Craig Gayle, wary of the invading detectives, leapt to his

feet, forced the tantalum sliver from Dean's constricting grasp, clutching it firmly, and was off, making a beeline for the toilets. Only managing to enter the nearest. The ladies. A metallic rebound as he whipped the cubicle door open. A hasty securing of the flimsy shell, only feet exposed. Paul Leonard, younger and faster, shouldered the door. It bent but stayed fastened.

'Open up. It's over, Gayle,' Paul Leonard garbled, bent over, face at the gap under the door. An echoing voice in that unsanitary sanitary provision. Nearly as unpleasant as the ammonia-stinking urinal next door. 'No escape, we've recorded your chat with Dean Wallace and—'

'And you ain't got no physical evidence.' Inside his metallic cage, his toilet closet, Craig Gayle ripped at the roll of toilet paper hanging loosely off the metal wall, enclosed the tantalum sliver, which threatened him and his liberty so much, and chucked the parcel down the pan. He grappled with a floppy handle yet managed a frantic flush. His package turned and twisted in the swirling water, and with one final whirl, it was gone. A sigh of relief.

Paul Leonard was fuming, well aware what Gayle had done. He lunged at the rickety door, which immediately caved in. Craig Gayle stood smiling in front of the toilet bowl; very pleased with himself.

'You cunt!' exploded Paul, and he grabbed Gayle by the shirt collar and hauled him, tumbling, out of the cubicle.

Warren Yates, standing nearby, was calm, calmer than you would have expected. True, they had Gayle's bleating confession recorded, but the bastard had trashed the crucial evidence. Paul Leonard held Gayle rigid, a policeman's official retaining clench.

'You are a moron, Craig Gayle,' Warren began, 'to think

we would trust our Dean here with such damning evidence. Evidence that you could get your dirty mitts on and do what you have just appeared to do. Oh no, you're dealing with people much smarter than yourself.'

Paul Leonard screwed up his face. What was he hearing? This was no time to jest, no time to relax. Crucial evidence had just been sent through the Thames Ditton sewers. Was his boss losing it? He found it hard to hold on to the struggling Gayle and hear such tripe.

Warren Yates became aware of his partner's pain. Another conjuring act. From that same scruffy brown envelope cradled in his deep pocket, with the same precise finger and thumb retrieval motion, Inspector Warren Yates produced a small tantalum screw, identical to the one now wedged in the sewage deposits of North-West Surrey. 'As I said, Dean Wallace was only allowed to flaunt a rough copy of the genuine evidence that was rescued from Golden Meadows. The last piece of your wife who you toasted in the crematorium furnace. Here is the actual tantalum piece that you searched for.' Warren held it tantalisingly near to Gayle's wincing face.

When you coax your brilliant nephew to produce an article, you ensure his skill is not wasted. You make certain, for the luxury of lunches, he fabricates two. Paul Leonard drew in huge gasps of air, wiped a beaded brow and knew this was another performance of police misbehaviour that he would have to swallow.

Craig Gayle couldn't believe it. His ploy of flushing away this vital proof had been in vain. He'd been outsmarted. A broken man. Paul Leonard felt Gayle's body work loose and slump in his arms, sagging in defeat. No longer the cocky confidence.

Down at the station, in the actual interview room, Craig Gayle offered no resistance, no excuses; simply a mumbled, slobbering admission. And there's nothing a policeman likes better than a slobbery confession. Chief Superintendent Collins-Maynard listened in to Craig Gayle's outpourings, a pleased man for once.

Back at base, well Kirsty Foster's home, several hours later, it was visiting time for the two detectives. For once, a celebratory atmosphere. Tea and detailed stories about the eventual success and Craig Gayle's final dribbled confession. But, for Kirsty, all these tales of triumph would not bring back her beloved Stephanie. Tom hugged Kirsty tightly as Warren and Paul specified all the recent activity, particularly the part played by Stephanie's finger repair and the tiny piece of metal that had ensnared the murdering Gayle, and how that finally brought Stephanie's killer husband to his knees.

'It has been you with your devotion to a dear lost friend who cracked this, Kirsty. Without your delving and research into Stephanie's injuries in France, we would still be chasing our tails or piling just another file too high to reach and with no chance of solving. This was your crusade, and it is you who has triumphed,' Warren gently declared. Leaving out, of course, his dubious role and the unlawful nature of the manufactured evidence. With many thanks for their persistence and promises of a quick return, the two officers were watched as they sauntered away from the Foster house.

Normality. Match of the Day. Tom was eager to see the goals. Kirsty, a woman's lack of interest, sought her computer. There had been little activity on the *For Stephanie* website and nothing on Stephanie's Wall. Now she could provide some closure. There was no need for further scribblings or memories.

Time to put this site to bed. Bury it, unlike what she would ever be able to do for Stephanie. In a brief message, Kirsty was able to inform her online friends of the final chapter of Stephanie's story. An extremely sad and tearful few paragraphs that brought tears to Kirsty's aching eyes. Response was almost immediate, horrified by Stephanie's awful incineration, condemnation of 'that shit of a husband', 'may he rot in prison', 'pity we can't put him through such a demeaning and mortifying ordeal'. And a rather lengthy message from Maureen Atkins and a promise to contact Kirsty with a FaceTime link.

Maureen echoed all the other notes from people emotionally broken by Stephanie's undignified death and disposal. However, she was curious, not in an interfering way, she had added, about one aspect of this dreadful business. It alerted Kirsty and broke her away from the stream of condolences. Kirsty read it again and again, slapping her cheeks in disbelief. Maureen was confounded by the role played by Stephanie's metallic finger repair. Kirsty was forced to read it aloud. And when the wobbly FaceTime image of Maureen Atkins came through, Maureen repeated almost word for word her scribbled message.

This is all too confusing, as I recall our day out of school accompanying Stephanie to Kingston Hospital orthopaedic department, where, several weeks after her skiing accident in France, the metal splint that had held her finger together was removed. Quite a vivid memory. The excitement of being out of the classroom, a dishy doctor. Stephanie wincing a little with pain. Paracetamol. Small stitches. No real complaints. It was definitely taken out. I didn't see it, but Steph said once they'd cleaned the blood off, it looked so, so small.

Kirsty eased Maureen off the active link, which allowed her to first become a stationary image on screen, and then gone. Kirsty was left looking at her own pained face and sat at the computer, baffled, dumb in disbelief. This was not a door she wanted to open. A deep swallow and some rapid movement. Dalton Riley had designed an easily navigated site. He had also provided, for events like this, an escape hatch. Kirsty was not going to disentangle this web of intrigue pitched by Maureen. Time for online demolition. First, Kirsty toppled the scribble wall, bricks tumbling, with comments seemingly flying off, whizzing in all directions. Followed by the album of photographs, images flashing forwards and then reduced to a mere dot, before a dying ping and were gone. Finally, Dalton had prepared the bugle sound of *The Last Post*. To which Kirsty's *For Stephanie* website, much like the beautiful woman herself, was sucked into a dark whirlpool, swirling with a burble and was no more.